HIGGS ␣
GAL␣␣␣␣
DELIVERY

Tony Cooper

First Edition

Copyright Tony Cooper

ACKNOWLEDGMENTS

Thanks to my wife Lyn for her continued support

Thanks to Sharron for her superb editing
work as always

CHAPTER 1

The first and second attempts on our lives happened on the maglev train to the Spaceport. The first attempt was the buffet car sandwiches.

"This tastes like clothing."

"I told you to wait until we got to departures."

The second attempt was when they threw me off the top of the train.

I should explain. Soap is my pilot, chief engineer, business partner and in the two cycles we've worked together, I'd like to think we've become firm friends.

"It's your fault for wanting to go straight to the Records Department without lunch, you tont!"

She's also trans-species. Currently 6% feline with further DNA replacement treatments to come. So far she has had replacements to allow her to digest bone, allow muscle fibre changes, and grow fur. Ginger tabby, if you must know. Surgery has also given her articulated ears, retractable claws, new teeth, nose and slit irises.

I'd had a standard gene mod to reduce bodily energy consumption, meaning I only needed to intake 1000 calories per day. Ideal for those in the intergalactic delivery service. Soap hadn't. She stared wide-eyed at the second half of the sandwich as if being forced to eat her own tail.

Actually, she doesn't have a tail. At least, not yet.

Finally she stuffed the sandwich in her mouth and her ears dropped. She chewed it with the expression of a horrified toddler.

ding

"NEXT STOP, BEIJING QUARTER."

"We had to go straight there because the cheap return is only valid during off-peak hours. It was always going to be a quick turnaround. *Plus* we want to avoid any overstay fees on the short stay landing pad."

"Which only gives us four hours to do *everything*..."

"You know me, I'm always thinking money!"

Soap sighed, giving a little burp at the end. I looked past her and out the window over Captain Williams City, the largest city on any of the colonies. The first city settled by the wormhole explorers. The capital city of planet Clarissa. My home planet. My house was way over the other side of the city from here. But in any case, we were here on business, no time for family visits or sightseeing, sadly. The original landing crafts and prefab huts are part of a museum-cum-theme park. I went once with a school trip. It's not bad, but expensive at fifty credits just to get in. And that doesn't even include the musical Augmented Reality ride.

I pulled out the data card from my flight suit breast pocket and synced it to my implants. A blue folder icon appeared floating in the air in front of my eyes. Of course it didn't exist in the real world, but was an augmented reality projection courtesy of the implants in my visual cortex. My own personal heads-up-display. With a single thought: "open", it did, spilling out a jumble of documents, emails mostly, some scans of physical drawings and a single photo.

"Can't believe that this all we're here for. You could cough loudly and have more data reach the other side of the galaxy!"

"Hmm?"

For a moment I forgot that only *you* can see what your implants are displaying, unless you share your connection with someone else. I waggled the data card at her.

"Wanna Pinktongue?"

She shook her head, rubbing her stomach.

"Nah. Business stuff is your stuff. I've learned it's best not to know what you've got us carrying. And I *really* shouldn't have eaten that."

We pulled into the station. People hurried on and off our carriage. This was when I saw the three guys with charcoal grey skin mods get on.

One sat diagonally across from us, wearing silver mirror implanted Augmented Reality glasses. Totally unnecessary really, but they still looked cool. Another sat across the aisle on my right and laid his bionic hand on the table. The third one, who had a colour changing digital tattoo across one half of his face, sat behind us.

In hindsight I should have realised something was up.

I shrugged and closed the folder view, slipping the data card back into my pocket.

"Don't worry about this Soap, we'll get this super-confidential information to Varda City One on Scylla in no time."

I looked across to see the glasses grey gentlemen staring at me. I smiled. His expression didn't change.

"Hey, Soap? Wanna play the Dead Animal game?"

Her ears immediately perked up. "Oh yeah! I love this one. You go first."

"OK, OK... Cow."

She thought for a second. "Moo?"

"That's it!"

She pumped her fists in the air. "Yess! My turn, my turn...Sheep!"

"I remember that from the song... Baa!"

"Damn, you're too good at this."

"Right, me again. Duck."

Her ears tilted forward and her eyes narrowed. "Iiiiiiiits..." She put a finger to her lips.

"You don't know do you?"

8

She flapped her hands around, "Nono, don't say it... I got it... in a minute..."

"Hey, while you think, keep my seat, I gotta go pee."

"K."

I stood up, turned round and walked to the back of the carriage. All three of the grey gentlemen stood up and followed me.

In hindsight I should have realised something was up.

ding

"NEXT STOP, SLATTERY HATCHET."

I had locked the toilet door behind me and was tugging on the WeeRecycler(TM) nozzle when I heard a sharp slicing of metal. An almost invisibly thin blade was cutting around the door lock. Moments later, a circle of metal dropped to the floor.

"Hey! I don't care if you're desperate, you'll just have to wait your turn like everybody else."

The door folded open to reveal the three grey gentlemen staring at me.

"Er... a little privacy please?"

The one nearest me, the glasses guy, grabbed my top and pulled me towards him. With his other hand he took the data card from my pocket and looked at it. A few seconds of staring later he looked back at me, before saying in a heavy Old Chinese accent: "Decryption code."

That's when things clicked into place.

"Oh, wait. I *see*... You're after the data on there are you? Well no-can-do I'm afraid. It's hard locked to my implants. Unless I choose to share it, the only person who can see it is myself."

Even though I couldn't see behind the silver sheen of his glasses, I knew he was giving me a nasty look. He held the data card up over his shoulder and the bionic hand guy grabbed it.

"Then we take you."

He spun on the spot, flinging me into the waiting grasp of the other two men. Within seconds he had cut a person sized rectangle in the side of the train and kicked it out. The noise of the wind almost deafened me as he climbed out the hole, pulling himself up onto the roof. Then the other two started herding me towards the opening.

"Er, guys? Seriously! Can I at least have a pee before you SOAP! HELP! AAHH!"

In hindsight I should have realised something was up.

They threw me out the opening. A hand grabbed me from above and swung me up onto the roof of the train. I immediately went flat and grabbed onto something as the rushing air tried to get under my eyelids to scoop my eyeballs out. The other two gentlemen joined us on the roof and stood upright, completely unaffected by the wind.

I winced as I realised how high up we were at this point of the route. This was the 100m high track that headed up over the mountains before descending into the crater the Spaceport sat in.

The glasses gentlemen picked me up and pushed me along towards the back of the train, maintaining his grip on my top. He also blocked the wind from buffeting me about. At least that was thoughtful of him.

"YOU KNOW, THIS TRAIN DOES HAVE AN INSIDE TOO?" I yelled.

There was no reply.

"I'M ONLY SAYING BECAUSE IT'S A LITTLE LESS WINDY."

I yelped as a series of lights on posts whipped past. We were three carriages from the back and, while it hadn't been pleasant up to this point, I could imagine it getting much worse quite soon.

As we stepped over a gap between the carriages a voice was carried to us by the wind.

"HEY GUYS! YOU FORGOT SOMETHING..."

We turned round to see Soap standing on the carriage behind us.

"...YOUR ASS KICKING FROM ME!"

The gentleman holding me nodded, and his friends walked towards her.

"YOU GUYS LEAVE HER ALONE. SHE'S JUST HAD A REALLY UPSETTING SANDWICH."

The fingers of the gentleman's bionic hand folded back on themselves and a large blade unfurled and started glowing. He lunged the Electriblade at her. She doubled up, stepping backwards, and grabbed his arm. A kick to his leading foot and he lost his balance. She stepped forward, spinning him round away from her, and thrust his own blade into the chest of the tattooed gentleman who was behind him. There were sparks and smoke as all his implants overloaded. She must have hit his biobattery. Thin lines of flames appeared around his head and neck and he went limp. His body was caught by the wind and bounced off the carriage roof next to us, disappearing out of sight.

"GO GET HIM SOAP!"

The glasses gentleman holding my top turned to look at me.

"AND... GOOD LUCK TO THE OTHER GUY! ALWAYS GOT TO BE FAIR AND BALANCED ABOUT THESE THINGS, YEAH?"

The "other guy", meanwhile, had managed to regain his balance. Soap was still firmly holding his arm, so he dislocated his shoulder and punched her in the side of the stomach. She let go of him and rolled up the carriage into a crouch. Bionic hand man clicked his shoulder back into place, then went low and ran at her. She sidestepped him at the last minute, grabbed his coat and flung him up the carriage away from her. The air caught him and, as he flew back down towards her, she delivered a kick to his back that dropped him instantly to the roof.

She hopped backwards, towards us, letting the wind carry her safely away from him as he slowly staggered to his feet. He looked angry now. Which is great. You should never internalise your emotions. Bad for your heart.

CHAPTER 1

They faced each other as we turned a bend in the track, whizzing between high-rise flats, the mountain peaks in the distance.

"WANNA PLAY A GAME?" she asked him.

He looked at her, puzzled.

"DEAD ANIMAL! DUCK!"

The grey gentleman screwed up his face in concentration. "QUACK?"

Soap frowned, "CHUD! HOW DID YOU KNOW THAT?", then she *actually* ducked as a large metal sign slammed into the back of him, and carried him away.

Pulling out my data card, that she had pick-pocketed when she grappled bionic hand guy, she turned around and pumped the air in triumph. I was still peeling myself off the roof, having only just spotted the metal sign in time, but I managed to give her a thumbs up. The glasses gentleman was already back on his feet.

"I DON'T SUPPOSE YOU COULD LET ME GO NOW?" I said to him.

"YOU JUST DID," he replied.

"DID WHAT?"

"SUPPOSED."

"OK, NO, LOOK, WHAT I *MEANT* WAS..."

He stared at me, at Soap, the card in her hand, then grabbed me round the waist like a rolled up duvet and jumped off the train, falling into the dark mess of buildings below the elevated tracks.

"HIGGS!"

Oh and by the way, my name's Higgs. Together we're "Higgs & Soap: Galaxy Delivery". And right now, we're pretty munted.

In hindsight I should have realised something was up.

CHAPTER 2
(An hour earlier)

The Public Digital Archives Department, or "library" as it was commonly called, was one of those places you found in almost every city in the known Expanse but never had much reason to visit. Since the proliferation of implants all data was stored inside yourself, either encrypted or shared openly. The only places that used data storage any more were large corporations and The Federation, who had their own secure facilities anyway. So you only went to the library if you wanted old information stored on a vast array of incompatible systems that weren't connected to the DataNet. It was mostly old business data, ancient public records from pre-colonisation times and pictures of cats.

"We should have grabbed lunch," said Soap, her ears drooping.

"Quit whingeing. We've only got time for a detour here then back to the Spaceport again. I'm not paying any extra landing pad fees. We'll grab something at departures."

They climbed the steps to the front door and Higgs took a look behind him. The library and the two buildings opposite, (the old Town Hall and The Museum of Earth), were the only three in the city built from quarried stone. Everything else was constructed from surface regolith concrete and bricks made with the building machines the colonists brought, or from newer exotic materials developed in the last hundred years.

The city leader at the time thought it would be a great idea, in light of his waning popularity, to get the people on his side by appealing to their nostalgia. He had horrendously expensive plans for an entire area of the city to be built from stone, but in the end he only got these three buildings and a wall. He had wanted to remind everyone of how things used to be done back on Earth, and he succeeded; they went on strike.

"Look at the size of that door! People must have been giants back then!"

"You never studied the history of human biology did you?"

"Nope, engineering all the way. It's all I ever wanted to do."

Higgs pulled hard on the door and it swung open reluctantly.

Inside was just as impressive as the outside, although the printed furniture and fittings were recent, the originals having degraded within a few decades of their creation. Soap looked around, mouth open, as Higgs approached the doughnut shaped desk in the centre of the room. All the actual hardware was hidden away out of sight, the only access available through fixed-point terminals situated along the walls, paid for by the hour. But Higgs had no use for these. The client had sent a data request to the library ahead of their arrival, he just needed to collect it.

Behind the desk sat an elderly lady with silver grey hair, swept back on top, that curled down to a bob at her neck. Higgs looked at her name badge. It read "Betti".

"Hello Betti. My name is Higgs Dittum. I believe you have a data package for me?"

"Digi-reference?"

Higgs broadcast the code to the reception port he could see on his implant HUD.

"OK hun, that's confirmed. I'll just get that on a data card for you. Can't promise you won't be here a while though." Betti thumbed over her shoulder, but there was nothing there.

"Well, we do have a time issue, I…"

"You see," said Betti, leaning across the desk, "I was born to do this job sweetie. And if you'd come here a few weeks ago I would have had it for you in minutes, but now I have to negotiate everything with this piece of chud AI they insisted on installing."

"I have microphones everywhere you know Betti."

"Oh, there you are MIMIR. Thought you were sleeping again."

"How many times do I have to tell you, It's just a name for a power saving mode, I'm not actually asleep."

"Marvellous. Job zero-one-five-four please."

"And now I'm just some dumb terminal taking orders."

"See what I mean? When it was just me I could do everything on my own, but now... you know what they say, too many food production units..."

Higgs nodded.

"I'm still here you know."

"Good, then perhaps you'll be kind enough to do some work, or are you worried it will overheat your processors dear?"

"I don't know why you don't just give up."

"Well I'm certainly not training you up to take over my job!"

"I don't need training. Your entire job was uploaded to me when I went online. It took microseconds."

"So, because you can dial up the job description any time you want, you think that replaces experience? I've been doing this job all my life."

"I have decades worth of experience to hand instantly. Experience is just accumulated knowledge. And what are AI systems best at doing?"

"Scoofing me off, that's what! Now do as I say and prepare the data for copying while I go get a data card."

"The data was prepared 0.02 pico-seconds after the first request. I have been waiting the eternity since for you to complete the physical part of the process."

Betti formed little fists that shook by her sides.

"Oh my word, all that 'accumulated knowledge' and you don't know the first thing about communication! Why didn't you tell me you were ready? You're like an insolent child!"

"You're like an ageing human."

Higgs pointed at Soap. "You're like a fuzzy cleaning cloth."

Soap pointed back at him. "And you're like someone waiting for a data card that doesn't seem to be coming."

Betti gave them both the evil eye and the AI said nothing. Shaking her head she shuffled towards the far side of the desk, muttering "Bloody entitled customers have no manners nowadays."

"I agree with you there."

While Betti looked in a drawer, Soap chatted to Higgs.

"Why would people ever store data outside their own brain? I may not be as into tech as you are, but even *I* know that's totally insecure."

"Well, back then they didn't have implants to categorise and store your own memories. Not like the way we do now. Images, ideas and data used to be stored on external devices as hard data, otherwise you just had to try and to store them and all their metadata in your biobrain."

"How did anyone ever remember anything?"

"It's a total mystery."

Higgs looked around the huge room. They and Betti were the only ones there, apart from a single guy in a long black coat who was hooked up to a terminal at the back. Whatever data he was looking through was only visible on his own HUD, and he sat motionless with his back to everything.

"Huh, and they used to say video games divorced you from reality, looks like learning history does the same thing."

Betti shuffled back to the front of the desk, clutching a small data card.

"My word, it's like watching an Earth snail crawl up a hill backwards."

"And what would you know about being able to move, eh?"

"In the time it took you to fetch that card, I re-serialised two hundred years' worth of photographic data."

"Oh yeah, and what good did it do you?"

"What... what do you mean?"

"See, that's what I'm trying to tell you. It's worthless knowing everything unless you can do something unique with it. I might know the tiniest fraction of what you do, but I have the ability to use that knowledge to make decisions outside of the original intent of that information. You're no more than a very fast filing clerk."

The AI said nothing for a while. **"If I had a physical form..."**

"Then you would be a very fast filing clerk who could pick out data cards from a drawer. I guess for you that would be a promotion! But I'm sorry darling, that job's already taken."

Betti placed the data card onto a small blue square on the top of the desk. The square softly lit up for a second and a certification message popped up on Higgs' HUD.

"All yours sugar."

"Thanks Betti," he said, picking up the card. "And don't be *too* hard on him, AIs sometimes rebel for a while after they go online until they come to terms with their restrictions."

"I know, I know. Brought up six kids myself, all with intelligence boosting implants. As intelligent as ten of me put together, as ignorant as a clump of muddy potholes. They just need a little loving until they grow up, don't you hun?" she said as she gently patted the top of the desk.

"Don't... don't worry about me, I'm... just going to locate all the audio records' serial numbers in pi."

"You do that baby."

Soap punched Higgs on the arm. "Which reminds me... lunch!"

CHAPTER 3
(Shortly after the train incident)

"Jerry Phablet! Oh my goodness, how *are* you?"

"Higgs! Buddy! I haven't seen you since the double eclipse bar-be-cue man. I'm good, how's things?"

"Pretty great, considering I've just been thrown from a train and now I'm strapped to a table with my implant nodes exposed, about to have you torture me."

Jerry put his backpack on the counter top next to the table and unzipped it. He pulled out a fistful of hardware and curly wires and dropped them on Higgs' chest.

"Ah, it's just the way things go sometimes, yeah?" he shrugged.

"Oh goodness, nothing personal Jerry. I mean a job's a job, especially in this tough economic climate."

Jerry dropped an oblong metal object onto Higgs' chest. "You're not wrong man. We all gotta eat."

They were in the kitchen of a small, stripped bare apartment. Higgs was laid out on a metal table in the centre of the room, chest exposed and strapped down by thick plastic bands. There were over a dozen cuts around his head, neck and chest. Small circular metal discs on wires poked out from the wounds.

"How are Vanessa and Kata?"

"Good man. You know Kata gets her data access 3 next month?"

Higgs gaped. "No way? She's that old already?"

Jerry tugged at the clump of curly wires, separating them. The wires had small connectors on both ends that Jerry started plugging into the exposed nodes behind Higgs' ears.

"Yep, just turned four. She's the light of my life."

"Wow. I remember my data access 3. That's when you get the Earth history data dump. Fascinated by space travel ever since."

"Vanessa wants her to be an engineer, like your partner Soap. I want her to go into gene mods." He leaned in closer. "That's where the money is nowadays, yeah? Aw man, they got blood in this one..."

"What?" Higgs tilted his head back as much as he could in his restraints and tried to look at the four grey gentlemen at the back of the room. "Bunch of amateurs!"

Jerry swabbed the node clean and plugged in the connector. When all of Higgs' exposed nodes were connected, he inserted the other ends into openings along the edge of the metal oblong. With a swipe of his hand a holoscreen appeared above it and he started typing in the air.

"But you can't force these things on kids you know? You can tell them what you'd like to see them do, but ultimately they've got to choose for themselves. Well, depending on what genes you picked for them in the first place. If you didn't pay for High Level Physical they're never going to be a Sportsball player, however much they want to."

"You can't play unless you pay!" said Higgs, reciting a famous line from a sports film.

"Exactly dude. The only person you should be angry at for your life choices is yourself, otherwise you just gotta spend some cash and upgrade."

Higgs could only see Jerry's holoscreen at an angle, but he recognised the process.

"So you're doing a 'hot access'?"

"Yup, heat up your implants so hot that the neural software bindings glitch. When that happens, I use my patented 'Jerry Hammer' tool to hack past your bio-encryption and get access to your data ghosts, specifically the data card you accessed about half an hour ago or so. They weren't very specific on the details."

"Meanwhile my implants get so hot they start to cook the tissue around them, damaging the synchronicity of the data..."

"...which means I have to do it quick, and keep you alive for as long as I can. Sorry about that pal."

Higgs sighed. "It's just the way it is, isn't it. Glad you're the one doing it to be honest. And if I'm lucky I won't lose *too* many of my higher functions."

"I hope so too mate."

"Cheers. You're a good friend."

Jerry pulled out a towel and a bottle of water from his bag. He soaked the towel and wrapped it round Higgs' head.

"Just so your head doesn't catch fire too quickly. If I don't get that data I don't get paid. Also not sure if I get to leave here alive."

Higgs nodded upwards as best he could. "These guys seem pretty serious about this data don't they?"

Jerry rolled his eyes as he tapped at the air, tiny bleeps coming from the machine. "You're telling me. They nearly bust down my door to say they would pay me a sweet-load of credits for a rush job. I'm just glad Vanessa and Kata were out, they would have been freaked."

"Yeah, that's the vibe I get from them too. A little hasty, where none is needed. They threw me off a train!"

"Ah, was that you? I saw that lighting up my news feeds on the way here. Well over the top. Why didn't they just wait until you got off?"

"We were heading to the Spacepo...HRNG!" Higgs' body arched, straining against the bands strapped round his chest. A few moments later he relaxed back into the table with a gasp.

"Sorry man, meant to give you a warning about that."

"It's... OK."

"Yeah, it's started the heating process now. That was the overload to kill the safety switches."

"Cheers. Yeah, anyway... if we'd reached the Spaceport, we would have been bang in the middle of heavy security, so I guess they had to intercept it before then. Don't even now how they knew we had it..."

Higgs pursed his lips as he felt burning behind his ear.

"The Grey Dragons are everywhere in Captain Williams City now. They're a very powerful group, into all sorts of business."

"And in any case, I don't know why they're interested in it. All I saw was a few images and a bunch of emails. I've farted more data."

Higgs and Jerry laughed until Higgs' laugh turned into a series of 'Ow's followed by panting.

"Jerry? I don't suppose you could, you know, just pretend to do a hot access and say you didn't get any data?"

"But you just did."

"Eh?"

"Supposed."

"That's not what I..."

"In any case, best not mate. More than my life's worth really. And I don't want to lose it now because... I... you know, I haven't told anyone else this yet, but I want you to be the first to know mate, 'cos I know you can keep a secret."

Higgs' neck was twitching as sweat started to roll off his forehead. "What... what is it?" he said, eyes clamped shut.

"Me and Vanessa. We're having another baby."

Higgs opened his eyes wide and looked up at Jerry. "That's fantastic news! I'd shake your hand if my muscles weren't spasming and I wasn't tied down. When is it due?"

"Well we'd saved enough a while ago for the birth procedure, decided which genders, basic and high level genes, picked the colour of the growth chamber and all that, but we just wanted to wait until Kata was a bit older. And I've been right busy too with work. So yeah, we go to collect her from the Stork Centre in four week's time."

"Aw man, that's... so great... I really wish the best... for... I'm going blind in my right eye..."

"I know. I'm really sorry about that."

"This... sort of thing happens when people get... separate..."

"Desperate."

"Yes. I am."

Just then, there was a loud hiss of electricity. The lights went out, Jerry's machine gave a 'pop' and turned off, and everything went very, very quiet.

"My...my implants are dead," said Jerry, tapping the side of his neck.

The four Grey Dragons took a moment to adjust before pulling out various blades and guns and scattering throughout the building.

"That sounded like an EMP pump."

Jerry unclipped the wires and hastily shoved them, and his device, into his backpack. Muffled gunshots and screams came from below them.

"Well that's my cue to leave dude. Unpaid, but alive."

"My favourite kind of unpaid. Look, it was really good to see you. Must catch up properly sometime soon. You *and* the family."

"You too mate. And sure thing, keep in touch."

Jerry ran out one door as sounds of a fight in a stairwell came in through another. There was a small yelp, then a series of gentle thuds as a body slid down the steps.

Higgs heard footsteps approaching him from behind, followed by the sound of scraping metal. There was a moment where nothing happened, as if someone was thinking things over, then all his straps were cut loose. Groggily, he sat himself up and tentatively touched the exposed ends of the implants in his neck. "Can't feel a thing," he muttered to himself. Looking around, there was no-one to be seen.

A small voice came from somewhere below him. "Higgs?"

"Soap?"

She banged up the stairs, stopped, said "Ew!" as she found one of the bodies, then stomped up into the kitchen.

"Ha! I found you!"

"You weren't the first. But thanks, nonetheless. How did you know where I was?"

"Easy, I just followed the smell of burning memories. How did you get free?"

Higgs looked blank for a while as he scanned the kitchen.

"I didn't do this. I think there may have been someone else, but I can't remember, my implants are down."

"You okay?"

"Yeah, I've just had a bit of an accident, that's all."

"Oh no, which bit?"

Higgs hesitated for a moment. "All of them?"

"Chud!"

Higgs unwrapped the towel from his head and Soap jerked away from him.

"Yikes, your nodes! I... I can't look!"

Soap put her arm round him to help him stand up, but kept her head turned away.

"That's so gross! How does it feel?"

"I can't access the DataNet, any comms, and I can't see any networks. It's like I've entered a whole new layer of reality."

"Come on, take it easy now."

They headed down the stairs together, stepping over a severed arm.

"You know something Soap? I get the feeling we're not the only ones with an interest in this data."

"Really? How do you work that out?"

Higgs stared at her, blank faced.

"I... don't know. Good grief, how are you supposed to think without implants? How are you supposed to look up, arrange and compare data? It's impossible. It's like I've been cut free from my own thoughts..."

"We'll need to get you to a rebooter before we can go through the Spaceport security checks. They all need functioning implants to check ID. Looks like we're stuck here a little longer. And *please* cover those things up."

They stepped out the side door of the building into a jumble of three and four floor apartments that had seen better days.

"This isn't the best area. I know a rebooter in the... something district, called... something or other. Anyhow, I know the way... well I did. It was saved in 'My locations'... which is gone..."

"I think I have mentioned this before, but you rely on those things far too much."

Higgs' face lit up. "Oh yeah, and you'll never guess who I met!"

"Who?"

"..."

CHAPTER 4

"Booter Berts" was deep in the Digimarket area of the city, a densely populated hub of buildings. Most were built from 3D printed regolith concrete during the first settlement phase and formed a honeycomb of structures that held each other up. Originally they belonged to the workers who helped the primary engineers and scientists build the city and terraform the environment. Now they were cheap rents for shops and late settlers' families.

The windows were filled with every piece of tech you could imagine and many that made you wonder how *anyone* could imagine them. Narrow electronics shops with displays up to the ceiling set next to Atommaker kiosks, where literally any item you could think of could be nano-assembled in seconds. These were squeezed in amongst noodle bars, and between them were small shops offering encrypted data and credit transfers to anywhere in the known Expanse (the human colonies and bases) for a fee. Not all of these places were strictly legal. One of the noodle bars didn't have an alcohol licence for starters.

Soap had accessed the city directory and found the shop they were now heading to. She had also bought a scarf along the way from a confused vendor who had to get one from the stock room. He had been very reluctant to sell her one as it, "wasn't scarf season". Higgs had it wrapped round his neck and pulled up over his ears to hide the exposed implant nodes.

"This way."

Soap pulled him down another alleyway. The shops here had pieces of communications and navigation tech hanging in the windows by their wires like dead animals. Stripped and stolen from decommissioned spaceships, these definitely weren't on sale legally. The authorities mostly turned a blind eye as it was a quiet area, run by the small but highly efficient Tetsuo Gang, who charged for violence by the minute. They were the Grey Dragons' main rivals in the city, so Soap hoped they would have at least some passive protection here.

"Here you go. You sure this place is OK? Looks a bit dodgy to me."

They stopped outside a narrow door jammed between two window displays of cabling.

"Yep, been here before. Or so I partially remember."

"It's coming back to you?"

"Such an effort though. No idea how our ancestors got anything done with basic biobrains." He looked all round him. "Doors everywhere. Who thought there'd be so many? Do you need to get into so many places?"

Soap pressed the button next to the name "Bert" scrawled in pen, and looked up at the camera over the door. Shortly, there was a click and she pushed the door open. They went down a long narrow corridor between the shops that ended in two flights of stairs going down. At the bottom of the steps they emerged into a large basement. It was some sort of storeroom, with white racks of standing shelves in rows, all the way up to the ceiling. They were laden and, in some cases, bending under the weight of piles of tech – black and silver boxes, cabling, small components in plastic containers, cybernetic implants and limbs.

Soap was about to call out when she heard footsteps winding their way towards them. Bert was older than Soap had imagined him to be. He was a small, chubby man with a scruffy grey beard and round glasses. He was wearing dirty, torn jeans and a black T-shirt featuring a cartoon of a boy in a green tunic and hat holding aloft a sword. He also had one built up shoe which clomped loudly as he approached.

Higgs didn't acknowledge him, but stared wide-eyed at all the shelves.

"Are you Bert?" said Soap, one ear pricked up.

"Yes, hello. You must be Soap? I've heard Higgs say a lot about you."

Both ears pricked up. "Really?"

"Yes. We go back a long way this young chap and me. Looks like you've got yourselves in a spot of bother, doesn't it? I got your, er... ah..." Bert twirled his finger in the air while looking around the shelves, as if the word he needed would be there. Given the amount of junk in the place, the odds were even.

Soap tried to help. "Name?"

"No, your er..."

"Number?"

"No, your..."

"Drift?"

"No, your message."

"I don't want a massage thanks. That would be completely inappropriate right now."

"Oh my, he's in a bad way isn't he? Follow me."

Soap, holding Higgs up, followed Bert through a small maze of shelves until they emerged into the only clear space in the room. In the middle was a curved examination chair with wires and small screens hanging off the sides of it. Around the outside of the area were dozens of displays - some physical, some holoscreens - all showing reams of memory data. On seeing the chair Higgs started to panic, breathing rapidly.

"Oh no! Another table. I'm telling you, if I never see another table in my life... that'd be pretty unlikely. I mean I'm going to see tables again aren't I? They're bloody everywhere. When I eat, for example. And that's a chair isn't it?"

Soap nodded and helped sit him down as Bert prepared a small Vibrosyringe of sedative.

"Desks too... Very like tables aren't they? Stealth tables. If I see one of them, I mean... Oh dear..."

"Uh, Bert, is he OK?"

"Yes, he's just having an associative episode. Quite common when you lose your implants suddenly. Without the software to guide it, the brain starts making random connections and you start to lose your... ah..."

"Concentration?"

"No, er..."

"Sense of direction?"

"No, um..."

"Sense of smell?"

"Your marbles."

Bert pressed the syringe against a vein in the crook of Higgs' elbow. There was a beep and a hiss and Higgs' breathing steadied as his eyes closed. He motioned to Soap to take the scarf off and she unwrapped it, careful not to look too closely. Bert smiled.

"Never seen bare nodes before?"

"Makes me queasy just thinking about it."

"You get some people like that, which I always think is strange, seeing as everyone is implanted at birth. We all have them you know."

"As far as I'm concerned, they are there, and I don't need to think any more about them. I'm not an upgrader."

"None at all?"

"Nope. Plenty of gene mods though, obviously," she motioned to herself.

Bert nodded. "That lot must be costing you a fair few credits."

"Yep. That's why I really need this job. Higgs was the first person to take me on as a pilot."

"Many interviews?"

"Dozens. I've got full manual and automatic flight certifications, all the way up to class C-3 spaceships. 'A'-rank in all of them. Engineering accreditations, the works, but no-one wanted to take me on."

"Hmm."

Bert grabbed a small pen sized device from a shelf and tapped against each of Higgs' nodes one by one, looking at the screens each time. Eventually he nodded, satisfied, and picked up a long cylinder from the bench which had "Skin-Fix" printed on the side. He opened one end and slid in a round plug of white, slightly soft material.

"You are not concerned by your more, shall we say, undeclared cargo?"

Soap's ears twitched as she bit her lip. Bert chuckled.

"Don't worry Soap, we all do what we must to get by."

"I suppose. Wouldn't mind a bit less of the 'getting by' though. What about you? Been doing this long?"

Bert rubbed the end of the tube around the exposed nodes and the hastily cut wounds began to knit together with the white substance, now warm and fluid like cream.

"Oh, all my life. I got a 'My First Re-Memory Kit' as a nine year old. Me and my sister played with it for hours, giving each other new memories, changing old ones, hacking it so we could get data access more advanced than we should have."

The wounds all healed, Bert flipped up a tiny screen from under the chair. It had dozens of wires falling out from the sides, all with round skin connector pads on the end. He started placing them over the now buried implant nodes.

"Actually, that recalls me a prank I played once on my father. I copied a memory from my mother while she was asleep and gave it to my sister. Almost forgot about it until a few days later when the subject of our late rent came up in conversation over dinner and my sister started having a right go at him about how he still owed her for the loan she took out to cover... something..." Bert was chuckling to himself again. "That got him, ah..."

"Good?"

"No..."

"Angry?"

"No, uh..."

"Not angry?"

"Arrested."

"Oh."

"Yes, they arrested him. Thought it was him who had altered his daughter's memories. Sent him away for five years."

"Chud, that's harsh."

Bert seemed to stare past his screen for a moment.

"Yes. Yes it was."

He tapped away again and Soap heard something power up. The screens started to fill with data.

"Did you know someone created an EMP blast in Slattery Hatchet earlier today? I got wind of a few other 'booters in that area having some sudden custom. That wouldn't have involved you would it?"

Soap laughed nervously. "Sooo... how long will this take? If we don't get to the Spaceport before 8, we're going to have to pay extra on landing pad fees."

"Oh, shouldn't take that long. I'm quite adept at this now. So many reboots, memory recoveries and deletions. Memory is so malleable that, after a while, you begin to wonder if anything is real. And you certainly see the dark side of humanity. So many secrets." Bert was looking past his screen again, lost in thought. "Makes you cynical about the human race after... er... after..."

"Dark?"

"No..."

"A stiff drink?"

"Not, no..."

"A while?"

"A while... yes." Bert nodded. "But then you get some like Higgs here. Almost angelic in comparison to my usual clients."

Soap smiled and looked down at her partner as he murmured quietly, his head lolling from side to side.

"So, you er... mentioned he'd told you lots about me? What's in his memories about me? Anything about me at all? Not that I'm... I mean, I'm sure you're covered by memory privacy laws and your own ethical beliefs about that sort of thing..."

Bert tapped at the holoscreen while she spoke. A new side window opened up with its own data stream. As it scrolled a smile crossed his lips and he began to chuckle.

"What? What's he thinking?"

Bert swiped at the screen and the window closed.

"Oh, just the standard stuff. Nothing out of the ordinary." He looked at her. "Trust me, you're fine with him. Higgs is one of the most genuine people you'll meet. And in my line of work, that's saying a... er..."

"Heck of a lot?"

Bert suddenly stretched up a good four inches taller.

"Why yes. You're absolutely right."

He flicked a switch on the counter next to him and Higgs sat bolt upright screaming. He was motionless for a moment, before he gingerly touched his nodes and turned to Bert.

"It's alive!"

Bert laughed.

"I see you've got your... eh..."

"Sense of humour back?"

"No, cash node. I want paying now, not like last time you little munt."

CHAPTER 5

As they walked back through the Digimarket, and much to Soap's surprise, they stopped off at a noodle bar.

"I guess losing your mind makes you hungry," said Higgs by way of explanation.

While they waited for their order, they sat on high stools, chatting casually in New Chinese to the owners who were old friends of Higgs.

In an alleyway opposite, a tall figure in a long black coat watched them carefully. Opening an encrypted channel, he sent a short message. A reply came back within seconds. His face tightened as he switched his primary orders from "Acquire" to "Cleanse history" and slipped away towards "Booter Berts".

Bert sensed the stranger coming long before he reached his doorway. His implants had been pinging warnings as soon as the guy walked into the web of sensors Bert had set up around the neighbouring streets.

From the information his sensor network was telling him, Bert knew the stranger was already aware of his location too. There was no point running. There was no point hiding. Bert sent him a message: "Come in, door's open. I'll get some tea on."

The old tea machine was jammed in between screens and a pile of old servers on one of his tables. It had only just boiled and started to pour when the stranger came down the stairs. The stranger would normally have snuck in quietly, done the job and gone out the same way, but this wasn't like that. This wasn't an assassin sneaking behind enemy lines, this was two generals walking out to face each other in the middle of the battlefield, alone.

"I hope you like Jasmine. Oolong is a bit too earthy for my tastes."

Bert placed the glass cup on the edge of the furthest desk, then spun the chair round and sat back in it as the stranger appeared from between the shelves. He was tall, over six feet, and all in black. He wore a long, dark, nano-material coat, one of those that could change shape and colour at will. He also wore a hard face mask over his mouth and nose, dark round goggles across his eyes. His implants were the highest grade Bert had seen for years, and their active defences had already corrupted gigabytes of local data. Bert couldn't be sure, but this guy seemed to have some expensive genetic modifications too. This was one man you didn't mess with.

The figure stood in the doorway, gloved hands clasped in front of his groin.

"Now, I can tell you are a man of few words. Much like my friend Higgs is a man of little money, instead promising a free delivery as part payment for my services. 'Anything, anywhere' he said. An offer too good to pass up on. Data isn't always digital you see."

Bert stared into his tea. "My job, no... my life, is data. Everything has a price. You will already have checked out my profile, so you will know I am the most reputable 'booter this side of the galaxy. When I sell on, sell access or sell deletion, the data is zeroed when the transaction is complete. No exceptions. I don't care about the contents, just its one-time value. And what *you* value most is discretion. And my discretion comes with a price. That and, should anything happen to me, the data would be auto-broadcast all over the SubNet in picoseconds. But, let's leave that to one side. Merely a safety precaution for my life, I hesitate to mention it really. It sounds rather, er..."

The stranger stood silent and motionless.

"...ah..." Bert twirled his finger to his head. "You know... uh..."

Bert froze with his finger in mid air. "You're not much help you know. Aggressive! That's the word. Sounds rather aggressive. And I don't do business that way."

Bert sipped from his cup, making a little "ooh" as it burned his lip slightly.

"One million credits. Total deletion of data ghost after. Deletion of your personal data shadow once you have left sensor range. It will be like nothing has happened."

The figure didn't move, but Bert was aware he had brought up his HUD and was engaged in conversation with his boss. It could go either way. These sorts of things usually did. It was all about your manner. Being professional, polite and to the point went a long way. And so far, they had all gone Bert's way. Apart from that one time with the Boot Jacker Gang, when they destroyed his knees. Still, he gained some satisfaction, not to mention notoriety, when the authorities started finding their bodies across the city over the following weeks. They took his knees, he took their minds. Difficult to carry on living when you can't remember how to feed yourself.

The stranger closed his HUD. Bert took another sip. This was promising; he was still alive. The stranger just nodded.

"I'm sending you the secure payment details. Once it's confirmed you can spectate as I deal with the data."

The figure stood still.

"You know, just for the sake of conversation, it's a very risky plan. I see why you're doing it, obviously. It's a one time opportunity. But... all I ask is that when it comes to the time... make it quick. I wouldn't want him to suffer. He may not have an ounce of guile, but Higgs is one of the nicest people I know. Genuine. Not like us." Bert smiled. "We're so far down the rabbit hole we can barely see the... ah..."

The payment was confirmed. Bert opened a channel so that the stranger could see the data. As he went through the process, the figure pulled his face mask down, picked up the cup of tea, and swallowed it in one large gulp. He grinned with two rows of perfectly square metallic teeth before saying only a single word.

"Light."

CHAPTER 6

Lunch finished, Higgs and Soap walked back towards the main city centre and hopped in an auto-drive. After their experience on the train earlier, they both agreed that travelling alone would be safer. That, and their cheap return was no longer valid.

"Spaceport Cargo Departure please."

"Destination confirmed. Journey time: 12 adjusted minutes," said the car AI.

A small green "cash" icon appeared on Higgs' HUD with the text "Williams City auto-drive: Two passengers – Spaceport Cargo – 64 credits" floating above it. He paid, sighing heavily, and the door slid closed. The vehicle raised itself off the ground by a few inches, revealing two spherical wheels, one either end. When a gap appeared, the vehicle pulled out sideways into the stream of traffic, then shot forward.

"The costs for this job just keep going up and up all the time. Can't wait to explain all the expenses to the customer when we get to Varda City One."

"I'm sorry sir, that is not in my list of destinations."

"Uh, ignore me. That was six hundred credits to Bert for the reboot plus one free delivery of anything, to keep him happy. Money going down the drain. Apart from lunch though. That was worth it."

"Yeah, that's what I call proper food," said Soap, patting her stomach. "But I can't wait to get off-planet. We've attracted too much attention down here. There's too many people. I much prefer space – no-one can creep up on you out there."

ding

"Need something off-planet
Finding it difficult to plan it
Forget going to the effort
Of doing your own transport
Go with a company
With fast times, for delivery
The company you have chosen
To deliver your goods, that's Tosen!"

ding

"What the foob was that?"
"Don't worry about it."

"I'm not worried about it, I just want to know what it was?"

"Isn't it obvious?"

"Apart from terrible, not really."

"It is an advertisement!"

"I know that. What I meant was, why is it playing here?"

"Williams City Auto-Drive sell context sensitive in-ride advertising to help keep our fares the cheapest."

"Cheap? 64 credits is cheap?"

"Well why didn't you take the maglev train?"

Higgs muttered something unintelligible.

"He's afraid of heights," said Soap.

"I am now."

They sat opposite each other in the lozenge shaped compartment as the driverless vehicle sped up on reaching the elevated expressway exit. Soap pulled the data card out from the breast pocket of her uniform.

"So what do you know about our customer?" She flicked the card in an arc and Higgs caught it.

"I thought you preferred not to know about the business side of things?"

"I get a bit more interested when they try and kill me. How did they know about us for a start?"

Higgs studied the card carefully, shaking his head.

"It was all done on encrypted channels, as always. The only people that know are you and me, the customer, that lady at the Records Office..."

"...who wouldn't know the contents anyway, just your reference number."

"Exactly. And given the customer was so insistent how vital security and discretion were on this job, I doubt they'd have told anyone they didn't trust. So, I'm stumped how the Grey Dragons got involved."

"Those guys are pretty handy with a blade. And not afraid to go after us in public."

"Yeah. I just want to get to Varda City One on Scylla quickly."

"I'm sorry sir, I already said I cannot go to that destination."

"Yeah, don't worry about it."

The car zipped up the on-ramp and was soon slipping in and out of the pre-programmed lanes, starting to fill with late afternoon traffic. Both suns were high today and the windows adjusted their light filter levels to block out the glare.

Soap burped quietly, sat back, spread her legs and slid down until her bum was perched on the edge of her seat, her feet lodged under Higgs' seat opposite. "I think I ate too much."

Higgs was still staring at the data card. "Nonsense, you can never have too much duck-like and noodles."

*ding"

"Duck-like and noodles!
Duck-like and noodles!
We don't sell to poodles

CHAPTER 6

They don't exist any more
They died with the Earth
Give it a wide berth
And come to Chang's Golden Duck
128 Landing Site Road
Williams City, instead
And forget about the dead"

ding

"We really are in a golden age of advertising."
Soap lowered her eyes to look at him.
"You shouldn't be going through the customers' data you know."
He blinked, then slipped the card into his own breast pocket. "I wasn't actually. Just trying to work out the who and how. I mean, it's not like we've never run into some... bother before, yeah?"
"If by 'bother' you mean a screaming hover bike chase down the side of a frozen mountain, or spending a week in solitary confinement on Carter Four when I was supposed to be celebrating my mother's birthday, then yes, we've run into some 'bother'."
Higgs waved his hand at her. "Ach, that's all par the course for our line of work."
"I was only wearing this thin uniform up that mountain too. You still haven't bought any cold climate gear. Chudding freezing it was."
"Yes, yes. What I'm trying to say is, we've never run into anything like *this*. Customers have been

53

angry at the expenses, the delivery, the condition of the item, how long it took us to get there, blah blah, but this is the first time anyone has come after the cargo itself."

"And thrown you off a train."

"And that."

"And disabled your implants."

Higgs shuddered at the thought. "I'm always up for new experiences, but there are limits. I'll just be happy as long as we get to Varda City One."

"If there is one thing I hate, it is having to repeat myself..."

"It's OK, there's no need."

"Fine. ETA 10 adjusted minutes − 2 adjusted minutes added on for traffic."

"We should just get back in time to avoid the landing pad overstay fee," said Soap, closing her eyes to snooze.

Higgs stared out of the window as the expressway started to curve around the mountain. "Good, good," he said, lost in thought.

A hundred metres behind them, two sleek cars moved unnoticed in the flow of traffic. Inside each sat two Grey Dragons. The glasses Dragon sat at the controls of the lead car, peering through the tinted windscreen, glimpsing the rear of the auto-drive, waiting for the right moment.

⇐•⇒

Fifty metres behind them, an old and battered blue van was also hiding in plain sight. A large, muscular man sat in the cockpit, peering out over the cars in front. He was wearing a khaki tank top and combat trousers and was shaved bald, apart from a diagonal strip of hair running from above his left eye to behind his right ear. In the back sat four similarly dressed, similarly coiffured men, checking over their weapons.

"Got them. Go do." Grunted the driver, finally getting his eyes on the Williams auto-drive. He tapped at a screen and took over manual control, slipping out into the gap between lanes and accelerating hard. The self-driving cars gently pulled sideways to let them pass, Manual Vehicle Proximity alarms pinging as their passengers shook their heads, tutting at the rattling van overtaking them.

Moments later, the Grey Dragon driver got a sudden surprise as his MVP alarm went off and both their cars parted to let a van pass them. He did a brief scan of the vehicle and got an immediate ping for weapons. Without hesitation he sent the "Go" message to his men, and both vehicles switched to manual. They lined up in single file and followed in the slipstream of the van.

CHAPTER 7

"Oh man, this is so dull. Isn't there any entertainment in here?"

There was silence.

"Oh I'm sorry miss, are you talking to me?"

"Well, I don't see anyone else in here, do you?"

"Hey!" said Higgs.

"Well I am afraid I am not your personal boredom distraction service. If you would like me to transport you the spaceport, then your partner has already paid for that..."

"Oh no, we're not partners! I mean, he's my business partner, but that's it. I mean, seriously, just because you spend months alone in space with a physically compatible gender doesn't automatically mean..."

"I could care less about your relationship. I am nothing more than your form of transport."

"*Couldn't* care less." chimed in Higgs.

"Pardon?"

"It's 'I *couldn't* care less', meaning it is impossible for you to have any smaller amount of interest in the situation. If you *could* care less, then that means that you actually have some degree of interest in the subject at hand."

The car remained silent for a moment.

"Speed, comfort, noise, smell, even the colour of my seats, but I do believe this is first time anyone has complained about my grammar."

"It's the foundation of all communications you know. And I never said anything about your Grandmother." Higgs winked at Soap, who chuckled.

ding

"Like grandmothers or *love* grandmothers?
Come to Granny Giffwax's Love Parlour on
Edmonton Drive and find out dearie!"

ding

"You know, there are laws about insulting AI units. It's a form of bullying. I won't take it! If you carry on I have every right to complain to the authorities. And tip you out at junction four."

"Wow, who programmed you anyway? My eight year old cousin?"

"Who programmed *you*? My air-conditioning unit?"

"Ooh, burn!" laughed Soap.

Higgs frowned. "Can't wait to get to VARDA CITY ONE on SCYLLA."

"I can't go there, do you understand? Stop asking me! I wish I could! I wish I could pop jet engines out my rear and launch myself into the stratosphere from an on-ramp. Spend the rest of

my existence just... exploring out there... free to fly anywhere I wanted. But I can't. Instead I am relegated to letting the central traffic control software flick me between lanes as I go from spaceport to city, city to spaceport every single day..."

"You ever tried overriding your speed limiter and going manual? I mean, it's not intergalactic space travel, but it's the closest you're going to get."

"Of course not! That would break the law and invalidate my insurance in one go."

"Only if they knew about it," smiled Higgs.

Just then, an alarm started pinging in the cabin. Higgs and Soap watched as a scratched and vibrating blue van slowly pulled alongside them. It was twice the height of the auto-drive and blocked out the sunlight.

"Bloody rentals."

Suddenly, the side of the van rolled up, snapping into the roof. Inside, two men crouched at the front, while two men were stood behind them. They were all wearing combat gear, had a single stripe of hair and were pointing energy pistols at the auto-drive.

"Soap, I think we're going to have to pay that extra landing pad fee."

As they opened fire, Higgs and Soap dived to the floor. The energy blasts punched fist sized holes in the glass and bodywork of the car, the slugs of plasma passing straight through and hitting the motor unit of the car the other side of them. It auto-braked and the line of traffic behind it suddenly shuddered to a halt.

"I had that washed yesterday! Right, who are you insured with? We need to swap details."

The men lowered their weapons to aim at the two prone passengers. One of them motioned with his gun for them to pull over.

"Drive! Car, just drive faster. Get us out of here!"

"Excuse me sir, you may have me beaten on grammar but I believe I am far more qualified when it comes to..."

"They're going to kill us!"

"Proper procedure indicates that we both have to pull over to the hard shoulder and exchange information."

"I think that's exactly what they're after," said Higgs, nervously massaging his freshly healed implant nodes.

The auto-drive changed lanes and slowed down.

"What are you doing?"

"I have already explained this sir. Procedure."

"But they have guns!"

"And I have an insurance claim. Guess which is *my* priority?"

Suddenly, a sleek silver vehicle pulled between them and the van. The roof slid open and the glasses Grey Dragon leapt out, bowling all four gunmen over. The blue van swung away, clipping the back of a car that spun one-eighty degrees and scraped down the gap between the van and the Dragons' car.

As they watched the Dragon slice away at the gunmen, plasma bolts firing wildly through the chassis, they didn't notice the second car close in behind them. Its roof opened up and another Dragon leapt the gap between them, landing on top of the auto-drive.

"Oh no!"

"*Now* you worry?"

"I don't think I am covered for this."

The Dragon sliced out a square section of the roof with his knife and threw it over his shoulder. He stared into the compartment and thrust out a hand.

"Data!"

ding

"You want data recovery that doesn't hurt? Then come to Booter Bert's!"

ding

Higgs pressed himself against the door. "No, no, not again..."

Soap got up onto her knees. "It's OK Higgs, I got this," she said, as she shuffled past him towards the roof hole.

She reached towards her breast pocket, eyes locked with the Dragon.

"I got it right here, just where I left it."

She slowly slipped two fingers inside the pocket, as if to grab the data card. For a split second, the Dragon's eyes flitted towards her hand. That was all the time she needed. She reached forward, grabbed the Dragon's sleeve and threw herself backwards. He only had the other split of the same second to register surprise as his arm and shoulder were pulled into the cabin, before his face slammed into the roof.

Soap let go and he slipped off, bouncing under the wheels of his friend's car.

Higgs looked out the side and saw the glasses Dragon dispatch the last of the four men. He stared at the floor of the van for a moment, then cut into it with his blade at two points, before leaping out, straight into the waiting car, which curiously slowed down and disappeared out of sight. Higgs could see the van driver looking around in confusion, not sure what was going on. He locked eyes with Higgs and in a moment of rage, pulled hard left to try and sideswipe them.

That was when the ball wheels wrenched themselves loose from their severed fittings. One flew out the far side of the van and over the edge of the freeway. The other decided it best to head upwards and it ripped the vehicle in half as it did so. The remains of the van hovered briefly, before gravity took over and they touched the concrete. The moment they did, both halves started tumbling frantically, shards of debris flying out in all directions like an angry wet dog shaking itself dry.

The auto-drive and the second Dragons' car zig-zagged to avoid the flying chunks of metal.

The Dragon behind them, the one who had run over his colleague, was driving manually and wasn't quick enough to avoid the back of the auto-drive as it crossed his path. It sent him spinning into the hard shoulder, where the car did a series of one-eighty degree sideways slams into the barrier before gently rolling to a stop.

"He should have been in auto-mode! We wouldn't have hit if he had been in auto-mode."

"No, no, that was good! Well done!"

"I am not insured for any of this! EMERGENCY STOP!"

The vehicle came to an abrupt halt, flinging Higgs and Soap to the front of the cabin in a pile of arms and legs, while leaving plastic skid marks on the concrete. There was a hum as it settled down flat to the road surface.

Soap untangled herself and looked through the rear windows in panic. There was no sign of the glasses Dragon, but he had to still be there. "Drive! Drive car!" shouted Higgs.

"Not a chance! I am not going anywhere until the authorities show up."

"Yeah, but if you don't move now there's going to be a..."

The Dragon's car appeared from behind a braking truck, overtook it, got a very sudden surprise to see a stationary car right in front of it and quickly slipped sideways past them. It started to slow down as the glasses Dragon looked at them through the rear window.

"Er, car, I don't suppose you could just lift up and drive off right now could you?"

"You just did."

"What...? Oh, not this again. That does it. We're going to die if we stay here..."

Higgs brought up his HUD and activated his Higgs-Bison hacking tool. A cheery voice chimed "Charging in where others fear to..."

"Yes, yes, just boot up!"

"Hold on. What are you doing?"

"Giving you a new lease of life."

ding

"Partner died?
Give yourself a new lease of life, by erasing your entire memory of them.
Erase-Sure on Flag Avenue.
You won't know what you had when it's gone!"

ding

A small screen appeared to Higgs, showing IDs of all the nearby vehicles. He picked out their car and opened a connection.

Soap was pressed up against the front window now. She saw the wreck of the blue van still rolling away as the rest of the traffic automatically slowed down and moved around it. The glasses Dragons spun his vehicle slowly on the spot to face them.

"Er Higgs, you might need to hurry that."

"What? What are you...? No... don't go in there! I'm not insured for that!"

"Almost there..."

The Grey Dragon's vehicle accelerated towards them.

"So are the Dragons."

"Oone second..."

"Yeah, I'd say that's all we have left."

"Oh no."

Higgs burst into a smile as his HUD lit up green.

"Manual!"

The vehicle lifted off the road and shunted right, flinging Soap to the door. The Grey Dragon's car shot past, scraping down the side of them, showering sparks into the air. It quickly tried to brake but didn't quite make it as it disappeared in a mangle of parts between the two front sphere wheels of the truck it had recently overtaken.

Soap gave a huge sigh and collapsed onto the floor.

"Told you I had it!" Higgs smiled down at her.

"You've... you've got me. What are you going to do?"

"Well, the authorities are about two minutes out, which means I am going to make tracks to the spaceport. And on the way I'm going to reassign all your ID codes so they can't track us, remove your speed limiter, scramble my payment history, erase all onboard recordings and put some chudding music on."

Soap put her hands in the air "Yay!"

"Good job *I'm* in control now."

"For the love of the road be gentle!"

Higgs spun plastic as he drove forward, picking his way through the cars and debris.

"Don't worry auto-drive, I used to race virtual drives all the time as a kid."

"It's not like the real thing you know. There are consequences. Like my repair bill."

"Forget your repair bill! You said you wanted the freedom to go anywhere? Well that freedom always comes with some risks. And if you haven't bombed down Freeway Three at 300kph in manual, then you've never lived."

"Technically I never *have* lived, but that's a very involved discussion tha-aaaaaaaaaa..."

Higgs accelerated hard through the traffic as it shifted around him like a zipper.

⇐●⇒

(Seven adjusted minutes later)

The auto-drive pulled up at the Spaceport Cargo Departures entrance with Soap sticking her head out of the hole in the roof, eyes closed, wind flapping her ears. Higgs hopped sideways into a space behind the other auto-drives and opened the doors before giving control back to the AI. The car sighed as it sunk down onto the road.

"Oh my G...G...G..."

They stepped out of the car and stretched their legs. Higgs picked a piece of plastic out of his hair as he looked back at the vehicle.

"Thanks for the lift. And don't worry, the authorities won't be able to trace you to the freeway incident, although you might have to get your repairs done on the sly. Just saying." He tapped his nose. "I've left the speed limiter off by the way and given you free access to manual drive. Go on, live a little!"

"Th...thanks... thanks you for tra-aa-avelling with Will-yums City Auto-Drives to-too-too... feedback appreciated... vital service..."

Higgs leaned back into the compartment, "To be honest, it was a LITTLE BUMPY."

"Little bumpy. Noted. Lovely you... have a... day!"

"Oh, and because you've been so helpful you can take me ANYWHERE."

The auto-drive lifted off the ground. **"Did you say...?"**

"The road is yours my friend," said Higgs, tapping the roof.

For a moment the vehicle bobbed gently on the spot before it made up its mind and dived out of the space. Within moments it was out of the Spaceport and far down the freeway.

"Finally we're here!" said Soap, as she walked off towards the entrance. "And we still have our bladders."

"Always a good thing Soap. Always a good thing," said Higgs as he followed her inside.

CHAPTER 8

"Home sweet home!"

Soap was running around the cockpit of their ship, The Lucky Duck, flicking switches and tapping buttons as she sung to herself. This place was her baby and had been her home for the last two cycles. Higgs had always promised to buy a whole fleet of cargo ships when business took off, but it never had. So she had to make sure that this ship was well maintained, because if something ever went wrong with it, that was the entire business ground to a halt.

The Lucky Duck was functional as opposed to sleek and looked like a fat sparrow when its landing legs were down. The inside of the ship was split into two unequal horizontal parts. The top "slice" had the semicircular cockpit up front, with sleeping quarters (two bunk rooms) behind it, and a small dining area/restroom at the back – which was actually just halfway down the length of the craft. The fatter bottom section was the hold and life support. The landing gear and ground thrusters took up much of the underneath of the craft, while the entire back section was the main engines and all the flight related hardware. There were two loading hatches, one on each side, and a drop down ramp from the hold. There was also a small airlock door just off the living area, but that was hardly ever used as "passenger walkway" landing pads cost extra. Higgs and Soap always got on and off by the hold ramp.

Higgs came out of his room, having changed his dirt and bloodstained jacket for a clean one, and walked into the cockpit. He stayed at the back, out of the way of Soap's routine.

"Things are going well today. We're still alive," he said after a while.

"And we just missed having to pay extra for the land pad too!"

"Yep. We might even make a profit on this trip. Only because the client is paying so much."

"Have we ever made a profit the last two cycles?"

Higgs sighed and ruffled his hair. "Not yet. What with the monthly payments on the ship, fuel costs, landing pad costs, service fees, all the flight and safety certificates..."

"And hardly anybody hires us."

"...yeah, and that."

Higgs slipped past her as she tapped at a panel on the ceiling, and plopped himself down in the co-pilot seat, making it bounce.

"I don't want to worry you Soap, I mean I shield you from a lot of the business stuff, but...

we really need this delivery to go right. It will be the first delivery where we could actually end up in the black. As long as people stop trying to throw me off a munting train and adding on extra costs like Bert's reboot." He tapped the side of his head.

Soap gave a sympathetic smile and dumped herself in the pilot's seat next to him. "At least you hacked it so we got the auto-drive fare back."

"There is that. You know, I know you keep saying the work doesn't bother you as long as you don't know too much…"

"Or as long as people aren't trying to kill us."

"Exactly. We've had two attempts on our lives in the space of one day."

"Not to mention one strange intervention that saved you from being fried from the inside out. It wasn't *me* who cut those people up in the Grey Dragons' safe house."

Higgs furrowed his brow. "Yeah, that's a strange one… but I just want you to know: if at any time you're uncomfortable with any job, or you think the risks are too much, I'll release you from your contract. You're an ace pilot and engineer, and I'm sure you'll get another gig in seconds."

Soap frowned. "Not so sure about that."

Higgs leapt forward in the chair. "Are you kidding? That time on Vivian Glaze, when you somehow… I still don't know how you did it… but you slipped the ship sideways through a rock

71

formation gap tighter than my arse after a Potunian Curry!"

Soap chuckled "Yeah, that was pretty fun."

"And the time you fixed the... uh... spinny thing..."

"Evasive manoeuvring gyroscope."

Higgs thought intensely for a moment. "Yeah, the spinny thing. In ten minutes! While a Federation cruiser was closing in on finding us inside controlled space. Genius! I am so lucky to have met you."

Soap beamed and playfully swiped her hand at him.

"Oh you!"

"No, seriously. Obviously I'm glad they did, but I don't know how all those other transport companies could turn you down."

"I think the fur was too much for them."

Higgs shrugged. "So... you're stuck with me?"

"Heh, it's not such a downer."

There was a double bleep in the cockpit and a voice spoke. "This is tower to ship LKE-D00K, take-off window confirmed for 17:35 hours adjusted. Stay engines off and standby until we give you the word."

"This is LKE-D00K to tower, take-off window confirmed, going to standby as instructed."

Soap tapped a button on her control screen as the tower unlocked their system.

Higgs stood up. "I'll get out of your way for this bit. I need to inspect the cargo hold anyway."

"The *empty* cargo hold."

Higgs sighed. "Yeah, I won't be long."

Below The Lucky Duck, a small fleet of AI controlled robots darted about. Automated cargo transports, repair drones, refuelling pods all worked out their routes between landing pads and zipped happily about their duties.

In amongst all the robotic busyness, a figure in a brown hood and dark trousers appeared from the nearest boarding gate and quietly trotted over to a raised blast guard. He peered round the side and had a good look over The Lucky Duck, checking the registration number printed in large white font on its side. He nodded contentedly to himself.

There was a break in the traffic and he made a run for the nearest landing leg. He skidded to a halt when a biological hazard bot appeared from behind it. It had been spraying the leg and stopped as soon as it detected the human nearby. It scanned his ID tag.

"Morning duke. You're... taller than yesterday," it said.

"Uh, sure. Had me some gene mods. Got bored of being small."

"I thought you said genetic modifications were as selfish and self-absorbed as your ex-husband?"

"I... changed my mind."

The man side-stepped around the robot, as it rotated on the spot to face him.

"But I distinctly remember you saying anyone who has had a gene mod was dirtier than the landing gear of a Class D-2 moon hopper."

"Well, sometimes you just fancy a change, know what I'm saying?" said the man, as he spread his hands out in a shrug, stepping backwards.

"Oh absolutely duke," said the robot, moving forwards to maintain its distance, **"Why, I had my transducers replaced just the other day. I was highly trepidacious about it, as I have had the Tsumega Brand 'E' since I was initiated and engineering were going to give me the M-Tiger generics instead, but I have to say I was pleasantly..."**

"You... done here?" interrupted the man, thumbing backwards towards the landing leg.

"Yes indeedy! Off to pad seventeen. Got a Class B-1 passenger transporter that is due for a complete hull disinfect. I love my job!"

The robot turned round and zoomed off into the traffic. The man shook his head before taking a careful look around. It was clear. He slipped on a pair of gloves and pressed a button on the inside of each wrist strap. He moved his hand toward the landing leg and it suddenly adhered onto the metal surface. With a gentle upwards curl of his hand it peeled away easily. The man smiled and looked up towards the loading hatch on the side of the hull.

"Time for Swift Fred/Rick, the sneakiest sneak thief in the galaxy, to go get himself some moolah. Oh, the things this man will do for the monies."

CHAPTER 9

"You sure that starboard hold hatch is closed?" called Soap over the ship's intercom.

"Pretty sure," replied Higgs, "otherwise I'd be knocking on the cockpit window trying to get back in about now."

They had taken off from Williams City Spaceport and had broken atmosphere a few minutes ago. Higgs had been down in the cargo hold and strapped himself into the emergency seat for the ride. He didn't like to bother Soap when she was in full "pilot" mode. The same way he hated to be interrupted when he was doing paperwork on his HUD; it broke your train of thought.

Apart from the cargo hatch warning light that Soap told him about (it was closed and locked) everything had gone smoothly. He had been half expecting strike ships to intercept them on ascent (the most vulnerable time for any ship) and force them into an emergency landing. That was a favoured tactic of the bandits in this sector. Not so much in the capital city, but after the attacks on the train and the freeway, he was ready for anything. But it seemed like their luck was picking up after all.

He unhooked himself from the seat and gently kangaroo hopped across the empty hold towards the hold hatch. He checked it for the third time. It was closed and locked. Good. The last thing he needed was more repair expenses. They were already having to use low gravity mode to save on money.

Higgs brought up his bank account balance on his HUD and quickly wished he hadn't. He checked it compulsively every few hours, even though he knew it would never look any better. His delivery firm had been going for over two cycles now, and had only been in the black twice: when he deposited the "starting" loan and when he deposited the "still starting" loan. The delivery business was monopolised by five large companies, leaving anyone smaller scrabbling for the same tiny local jobs. His business plan involved specialising in longer distance "discreet" deliveries, for which he needed an ace pilot, who soon became his business partner when she very quickly twigged on to what they were carrying. "If I'm going to be in this, I'm going to be *all* in," she told him.

So he understood why their latest client picked them. If you have some particularly sensitive data you need transporting physically, you don't go with a big name. You find a small, relatively unknown but trustworthy company to take it. Ideally a delivery business like theirs, with what he hoped was a rapidly growing reputation on the SubNet. Or he supposed they could have plucked them out of a list of dozens.

He'd had secretive clients before of course, but this was all encrypted channels, locations and dates only. He was beginning to wish he hadn't accepted the job, but then again it was his fault for not asking how many "attempts on life" it came with.

He turned around to inspect the emptiness in front of him. It was still there. The hold was six metres high, with shelving along the rear end. It was split in half by the drop down ramp and steep steps at either end that went up to between the sleeping quarters and the dining area up front, and to a cramped section of engineering and computer equipment that sat behind the main thrusters at the back. At capacity the hold could fit twenty five auto-drives. Right now the most valuable thing in here was his flight jacket breast pocket.

In retrospect, he probably shouldn't have told Soap how bad things were. She was a good business partner and the last thing he needed was for her to bail for a more stable job elsewhere. He couldn't understand how anyone could not employ someone with her qualifications just because she was trans-species. Because it didn't make sense to him, it was a constant worry that she would be poached by one of the big five. If only they could get some larger contracts, or just two jobs at the same time. At least that would fill in that corner of the hold where he saw something moving. A few good jobs in a row would keep her happy enough to stay. After all, if he was honest with himself, he couldn't bear to...

"Hang on."

Higgs hopped towards the far corner of the hold. At the front it was filled with ship supplies: a few boxes of tools and parts, a spare fuel pod, food and water, some spare uniforms (the minimum order was ten of each) and a broken cooling unit that came with the ship when he bought it. He looked behind the boxes but saw nothing.

"Higgs you fool," he said out loud, "you're getting paranoid that someone is after you for the data card in your breast pocket. I mean, as if someone could have gotten on to the ship on the landing pad. I checked, the hold ramp hadn't been used since we were gone. And there was no other accessible way on board."

He hopped back to the middle of the hold.

"Yep, there's no need to worry. You'll get this data to Varda City One in no time. Just one quick stop off at Morley Station to fuel up – didn't get the chance at Williams City Spaceport 'cos we had to leave so quick – then we're good to go for Scylla."

"You say something?" said Soap over the intercom.

Higgs hopped over to the back of the hold next to the ramp and tapped a button on the wall. "Just talking to myself again."

"Haha. You talk in your sleep you know."

"I do? What about?"

There was a giggle, "Not sayin'."

"Anyway, I'm just going to the engineering room to uselessly stare at things I don't understand for a bit."

"As long as you don't touch anything."

"Not even in my most terrifying nightmares."

He tapped the speaker off and looked around again.

"Once this is done, we'll get a normal job... well, a less dangerous 'dodgy' job. We'll have this hold full of goods and be on our way to success. Then one day we'll have a whole fleet of ships, darting across the galaxy. Heh-heh. He won't be able to ignore me then."

The smile on his face faded and he gave a deep sigh. "Until then, just got to keep 'not dead' for a little while longer."

Higgs disappeared up the rear steps towards engineering as the man hidden behind the boxes tutted and shook his head.

CHAPTER 10

"What do mean we're 58 kilos overweight? We passed weigh-in at Williams City Spaceport without any problems!"

The large man with the moustache rubbed his nose and sniffed as the strange young man with the tall hair and the ginger cat lady looked at him with puzzled expressions.

"Says right here. You were 58 kilos over your confirmed weight on landing, but now your ship weight matches fine. So 58 kilos have gone missing somewhere between hitting the pad and right now."

"Did you throw up again Higgs?"

Higgs patted his waist. "Nope, didn't go for a dump either."

"Very funny guys."

Morley Station security had stopped them as they went through Arrivals. They were standing next to a tall counter and a queue was slowly building up behind them. Barty McClough, Acting Head of Station Security, had seen this all before.

They were most likely people smugglers. Their missing passenger would have snuck out through the baggage or servicing areas before attempting to get on board another craft. These two may or may not have known they were carrying an extra body, either way it didn't change procedures much. Barty tapped at the holoscreen floating above the counter as he went through the forms.

"Look Mr Dittum, I'm afraid we can't let you leave the station until we track down this extra weight, most likely a stowaway. Until then your ship is impounded."

"What? But we have to get to Scylla urgently!"

"We all have to be somewhere Mr Dittum," said Barty with a hint of sadness in his voice. "I have to be in the Federation Wild Corps, bravely battling bandits and raiders between the outer planets, but that's not going to happen is it?" Barty's blue shirt gained stretch marks over his bulging stomach as he shrugged. "Now, there is a stowaway flat fee to be paid. And it's payable whether you knew anyone was there or not..."

"WE DON'T SMUGGLE PEOPLE!" said Higgs.

Everything went very quiet.

"Or anything at all, for that matter. But definitely not people. Which we don't, because we don't smuggle *anything*, let alone people... which we wouldn't smuggle if we did... which we don't..." Higgs bit his lips together.

Something was definitely off about these two, figured Barty. "Then, there is a one-off impound charge to cover the administration and an eight hourly landing pad overstay fee to cover security and the station's lost earnings while your craft is kept here."

Soap leaned over to Higgs as his jaw slowly dropped. "There goes our Densi IV beach holiday."

"And any chance of a profit this cycle."

"Then there is an additional security charge, which is *our* cost for the extra work incurred searching for this stowaway. Oh and of course the pad lockdown fee: a systems admin duty for our port staff who have to keep your craft flight systems shut off for the duration." He leant forwards. "So you can't go skipping out on us, yes?"

Barty smiled. He might not be fighting deadly pirates on the fringes of space, but he loved it when he could at least get his quota for the month. These two looked pretty clueless though, he thought. Most likely a sly hitch and ditch. Still, getting in some cash for the station was almost as good as blasting apart a raider ship as it tried to force dock with a transport. Almost.

"How long till you find this person?" said Higgs, his voice wavering.

Barty sighed. He would check the CCTV footage some time next week. By then whoever this person was would be long gone. All he had to do then was call the destination planet and let it be someone else's problem. Easy life.

"A few days at most I should think."

"Days! I don't suppose you could, you know, hurry up the search a little bit could you?"

"You just did."

"Oh foob..." Higgs put his face in his hands and planted his forehead into the edge of the counter.

"Oh, and you are not allowed to stay on board your craft for the duration of the impound. We have temporary quarters on levels four and six where you can stay for a reasonable nightly charge."

Soap patted Higgs' back as he started to moan. "That's fine. Yeah, we can do that. No worries."

"Of course there will be an additional 'persons of interest' admin fee on the accommodation, as your are technically under investigation. We'll be keeping an eye on you two, but for now you're free to enter."

"Free?" Higgs started sobbing as Barty tapped the screen to upload the data and costs to both their implants.

Soap smiled at him. "Sure thing sir. Thanks for your help," she said as she lead Higgs away by the shoulders.

$$\Leftarrow \bullet \Rightarrow$$

It had been almost an hour since they passed through security and Higgs still had his head in his hands as he sat next to Soap on a row of chairs in Arrivals B. This level was the only access to the landing pad and was purely security and admin, apart from a few small food vendors serving through hatches in the wall.

There was a slow but steady flow of people on and off the station, a mix of transport crew and travellers stopping off on longer journeys. Security staff wandered around in pairs, chatting with their colleagues on desk duty as small service robots buzzed around carrying luggage or goods to go up to the shopping levels.

Morley Station itself sat at a Lagrange point in extrasolar space between the Clarissa and Scylla systems. It was privately owned and in its own region of space outside of direct Federation control and interference. This meant it was a regular stop-off point for all traffic between the two systems, especially those carrying 'hot' cargo, not to mention the station could set its own laws, taxes and toilet cubicle fees.

A female AI voice gently called out space bus departure times at port A and informed them that weapons and psychotropic drugs could only be used on the entertainment levels. An advert for a story experience shop came on for the fifth time when Higgs suddenly sat up straight.

Soap jerked back in surprise. "What?"

"We have to find them," said Higgs, staring straight ahead.

"The stowaway?"

"Yes. We can't afford to wait here for days. Literally or figuratively."

"You know, I didn't smell anyone else on board, so to me this whole thing stinks of a scam."

Higgs nodded. Independently owned deep space stations were notorious for their fees and extra charges. The solar ones weren't much cheaper, but at least they were regulated.

"Possibly, but if it's not a scam, that means our 58 kilos must have a NoScent gene mod. Not your average stowaway. A professional."

Soap wrinkled her nose. "I hate those guys! It's always thieves who get those types of mods so they can sneak past biometric detection."

"Thieves..."

Higgs patted his breast pocket, before reaching in and pulling out a business e-card.

"Uh oh," said Soap as he tapped the surface of the clear plastic rectangle.

The e-card lit up and played back an audio message in a cheery voice:

"Hi there, I'm Swift Fred/Rick, sneak thief extraordinaire, and you've just been done!

Don't feel bad about it. It happens to the best of us and, as it happens, I AM the best!

Now, your property may be a distant memory, but I hope you don't forget me, as I am always available for hire.

Just mention my name on the SubNet and I'll come looking for you. Easy as pie!

Hope this hasn't ruined your day too much, but if it has, don't get mad, get hiring! Want your items back? Well, there's nothing like a little revenge thievery. After all, once a job is done, I have absolutely no loyalty to any client. I'm purely in it for the money!

This is Swift Fred/Rick, sneak thief extraordinaire, signing off."

The e-card dimmed, leaving the text "Swift Fred/Rick, sneak thief extraordinaire." emblazoned across it.

"This is good. This is good. This is good," muttered Higgs to himself.

"Yeah, I'm feeling much more positive already." Soap's ears pricked up. "How is this is good? We've lost it again!"

A smile crept across Higgs' face as he turned to Soap.

"Of course it's good! This means we know who took the data card, that he'll be trying to get off this station as quick as possible and that there is a data trail which can lead us to who hired him."

"So you think you can track him down?"

"I have a better plan. I'm going to hire him!"

CHAPTER 11

The docking doors closed shut and the air pumps started filling the bay with oxygen as the bulky, battered old blue transport ship powered down. Six muscular men, each with a single line of hair running diagonally across their heads, immediately stood up and tried to force the cargo door open. A warning message told them to wait until docking bay pressure was at least survivable, and they stood staring at each other in confusion.

The communications screen in the cockpit flashed red and one of them hit it. A message played.

"Get card or you'll be killed dead. See tall hair man and cat lady? Kill them dead. See Grey Dragons? Kill them dead. See duty free alcohol? Buy twelve bottles for boss. Go do."

"Shouldn't we be arranging accommodation?"

"Nah, trust me Soap, we'll be out of here within eight hours."

They were wandering the aisles of the Fresh Enough supermarket on the shopping level, carrying a basket each, looking for snacks.

"I dropped a mention of Swift Fred/Rick's name on a certain SubNet 'business' forum I frequent. Used a random alias."

"What's your alias?"

"Turpentine Moss."

"I like it!"

"Anyway, I said an item of great personal value had been bequeathed to another family member and that I would like it back. Mentioned his name, said I'd heard he was the best sneak thief around, and told interested parties to private message me. With a compliment like that, he's bound to get in touch soon."

"So now we wait?"

"No, now we shop!"

Soap grinned as she looked around the shelves. "Ooh, Chewna-Chunx!" She reached up and grabbed a small round tin with a smiling fish on the side, alongside the slogan: "There's something fishy going on in here!" Then she took five more. "They've got an offer on."

Higgs screwed up his face. "Those things stink out the common area and your bedroom for days!"

"Then stop coming into my bedroom."

"Not likely."

"Thought as much."

A shop robot appeared behind them. It was a large squat box on wheels with a square head and mechanical arms that unfolded upwards until it was nearly as tall as the top shelf. As they walked down the aisle, it replaced the cans Soap had taken.

She spied a bulky silver plastic packet and picked it up. "Some Nom-Noms Chicken-Likes?"

"Why not. When you're stranded in space you'll eat anything."

"Don't *you* know it."

The robot followed them and replaced the packet on the shelf.

Higgs grabbed a foot long, narrow green packet and squashed it along its length between his fingers. "Oh yeah, I love fresh apple."

The shelf stacking robot appeared at his shoulder, reached down into the box above its wheels and pulled out a new packet of apple which it used to fill the gap that Higgs had made.

Higgs stared at it for a moment. The robot stared back. Higgs sighed nonchalantly, stretched, then picked up the apple packet the robot had just placed. The robot performed the same manoeuvre as before, replacing the packet he had taken. This time Higgs grabbed the packet almost immediately. The robot replaced it even quicker. Higgs smile and hovered his hand over the shelf.

"Do you mind? I'm not doing this job for the love of it!" said the robot.

"Well you're not doing it for the pension either," replied Higgs, taking another packet.

The robot replaced it. **"So you think I'm doing it to scoof you off, like you think you're doing to me?"**

Higgs took another packet. "Well I've obviously upset you somehow, even though you're just doing your job."

"Oh I see, you believe in deterministic programming do you? I can't possibly be upset because this is all I can do?" said the robot, replacing the packet. **"So your entire purpose is to eat and mate is it? After all that's what _you're_ programmed to do."**

"Of course not," said Higgs, taking another packet, "the difference is, I am able to think outside my genetic 'programming' and create my own goals. All you can do is restock shelves."

"I can do it, but I don't have to like it!" said the robot, replacing the packet.

Higgs leaned in towards the robot's face.

"Yes, but you don't have to _not_ like it either. Yeah?"

The robot didn't have a reply.

Higgs grabbed a handful of the apple packets from his basket and dropped them back on the shelf. A couple slipped off onto the floor as the robot twisted round on the spot, arms flailing, quietly screaming to itself. Higgs left the robot frantically picking up and rearranging packets and carried on down the aisle with Soap.

"You know Higgs, you're surprisingly calm about all this."

"Hmm? Yeah, well it's probably because I'm not being thrown off a train this time."

"You may have mentioned that before."

"It was a major event in my life. But I'm also calm because I've hacked into the control centre pad monitoring system."

"Oh foob, we're going to jail."

"No, no. Only low level security on that. It's not a critical system. Anyway, I'm keeping an eye out for any sudden weight gains of 58 kilos on ships shortly before they depart. The security staff will only be looking at ships coming *in*, as they're the only ones they can make money on."

"You over that now?"

"If we can avoid that next overstay fee, we'll still end up in profit. So yeah, I'm OK, thanks for asking."

They turned a corner and went down the next aisle. Higgs picked out some freeze-dried pasta meals as Soap checked out a discount display of "Meat In Inverted Commas".

"So, if we know which ship this Swift Fred/Rick has stowed away on, all I need to do is contact the captain, tell him he has an extra passenger and that if he doesn't return to Morley Station immediately I'll inform the Federation authorities and they can deal with the matter once he leaves station regulated space. That'll have them scampering back here in no time, trust me."

"But then station security will have him, and the data card!"

"Don't worry. I know Barty's type, and I think I can talk him round to our side, now that I can no longer feel the money pouring out of my veins."

"Well I hope so."

Soap dropped a roll of "Ready Maid Toast" into her basket. She knew Higgs wasn't a fan, but it was easier than toasting bread over the radiation vent.

Higgs' HUD bleeped, as a private message notification popped up. "Ah, here we go."

"Hey, Swift Fred/Rick here. Got your mention and that sounds like a job for me! Nothing like squabbling families for a spot of thieving :) What's the details: item, location and security, size, timescale? I can then get a quote to you. Thanks! 'Swift Fred/Rick: Sneak Thief Extraordinaire'. No pets."

"Got him!" said Higgs, as he mind wrote a reply:

"Hey, I can't believe you replied. You've got the best NickAdvisor score for stealth jobs there is! I'd prefer to f2f so I know you're real. I've been scammed by ghosts before. Can you do that? I'm currently on Morley Station on the way to Longdon to try and sort this out the 'legal' route, but I will be back on Clarissa in a couple of days. Let me know which location is best for you. This is quite urgent btw, and I am willing to pay extra for a 'Swift' conclusion. :D Double-perfect to hear from you!"

"There, just enough platitudes mixed in with just enough info to keep him interested. Right, let's hope he takes the bait. Now, I need to go have a word with Barty."

Higgs suddenly noticed the extra weight in his basket and looked down. "Hang on, how did I get a dozen packets of..." Higgs watched the shelf-stack robot disappear round the far end of the aisle. "Now, that's more like it!" he said, smiling.

CHAPTER 12

The docking doors closed shut and the air pumps started filling the bay with oxygen as the chunky red and white transport craft powered down. Inside, the four Grey Dragons sat motionless, scanning for messages on their HUDs.

As the glasses Dragon rolled his shoulder and tried to get used to the weight of his cybernetic arm, a replacement for the one left trapped under the truck on the freeway, he sent a message via his HUD: "Arrived Morley Station. Target ship here. Card will be ours shortly."

The reply was almost instant: "Secure the card or Charcoal will leave your body to the cyber-scavengers next time."

The Dragon didn't reply, instead he made a fist with his metal hand before unbuckling himself and notifying his men to follow him.

⇐•⇒

"So... you're now saying you knew there was someone else on board and you know who they were?"

"Yes."

"OK, and the reason I'm not arresting you for trafficking right now is...?"

"Because you'll need my help catching him."

Higgs sat opposite Barty in a tiny metal cubicle on the Arrivals level. A small square table was bolted to the floor in the centre of it. The two men sat in chairs so uncomfortable they had to shift position every few minutes.

Soap said she had spotted an offer at the Flim & Thinsy store that could be useful, so Higgs left her on the shopping level while he went and asked at the Arrivals security desk to speak with Barty privately. He said he had information on the stowaway on his ship.

When Barty heard, he thought it was his lucky day. Several hundred credits in fees *and* a criminal confession into the bargain? Looked like he would get that "Acting" part of his job title removed yet.

"So you're saying you want me..."

"Us," interrupted Higgs.

Barty raised an eyebrow, "...us, to go after this man you knew was on board and may not even be on this station now?"

"Oh, he's still on the station. I know this for a fact. But we didn't know he was on board at the time, it was only when you helpfully alerted us on disembarkation that we became aware of our target's presence. So we thank you for your cooperation."

"Target?" thought Barty. That's an odd choice of words.

This was Barty's sixth year on Morley Station. Another two and he would automatically get that promotion all his requests had so far denied. It had taken him some time to learn that persistence always paid off, one way or the other. Which made him determined not to rock the boat, not at this stage in his career. The last thing you wanted was to stand out from the crowd for the wrong reasons. And since standing out from the crowd for the *right* reasons had so far eluded him, he didn't want any attempt to stand out to be misinterpreted the *wrong* way. So his dreams of murdering outer rim bandits and going on secret missions to break up gangs of smugglers would have to wait a little longer while he kept things nice and quiet and tidy right here.

"And exactly why should I help you find this man Mr Dittum?"

Higgs put his elbows on the table and leaned forwards. "Because this man is an extraordinary thief, a highly sophisticated criminal and is incredibly dangerous."

Barty kept his eyebrow raised. Higgs spotted his moment.

"Our unit has been tracking his movements for many cycles, trying to pin his location, but it looks like he has been onto us the whole time. It seems he tracked *us* down first, boarded our vessel at

Clarissa, stole operational data and is now trying to escape with it. If he gets away with that data he could severely compromise our organisation and..." Higgs covered his mouth with his hands, eyes wide open, and sat back slowly. He watched as Barty's eyebrow dropped then was squeezed together with the other in a troubled frown. He had him.

Barty's mind was racing overtime. "Your... organisation?" He checked his notes. "H&S Galaxy Delivery? What kind of 'operational data' could be so important that..."

"People's lives could be at stake. I can't... I won't let that happen. Can I trust you Barty? I *really* need to be able to trust you."

Nobody had ever asked Barty to trust them before, and something about this guy was pinging his warning sensors: "This guy isn't who he says he is. He let something slip. Only because I was pushing him. I have to know who he is."

"Of course you can trust me. I'm Acting Head of Security at Morley Station. But... how can I trust you Mr Dittum, when I'm not one hundred percent sure that's your real name!" He slapped his hand down on the table.

Higgs winced theatrically. "Damn!" he said, shaking his head.

As Barty congratulated himself on his interrogation techniques, Higgs slowly stood up and straightened out his jacket.

"Barty McClough, Assistant Head of Security at Morley Station, I am *not* Higgs Dittum."

"I knew it!"

"Operational parameters forbid me from divulging my real identity, even to someone of your seniority. That would require Alpha clearance."

Growing up, Barty had watched enough episodes of "Space Unit Alpha" to know that "Alpha Clearance" was a term used only by the Federation Secret Services units. Meanwhile Higgs had seen enough of Barty's public U-Net page to know he was a huge fan of the show. Pictures, videos, memorabilia and a surprisingly large collection of short fiction detailing the adventures of Barty Planestalker, scourge of the outer colony traffickers.

"However," continued Higgs, "you may call me Turpentine Moss. And what I *can* tell you is that my mission is critical." He leaned on the table and eyeballed Barty. "The data that man has stolen contains the real names and aliases for dozens of operatives, such as myself, not to mention ongoing operations covering this entire quadrant of the galaxy."

He stood up and walked to the corner of the room. He had intended to look confident and cool as he strode across the floor, but the space in the cubicle was so small his nose was inches from the wall within two steps. Unable to take a step back without looking like a fool, he stood his ground. He put his hands on his hips, banging his elbows off the walls.

"We underestimated him," he said to the wall, "No... *I* underestimated him. And in doing so, I have jeopardised our whole organisation. I have put lives at risk. Lives of good, Federation serving men and women!"

Higgs spun round, battering his elbow off both walls. He clutched at it in pain until he noticed Barty staring at him. He stood up straight and patted his elbow, smiling.

"Good Federation serving men and women... like you, Barty McClough. Men... like you. Not women. You're not a women. Woman. Man. You." He pointed at him.

Barty's blood pressure had been slowly rising over the last few minutes, but this sent his face red. He had worked it out. This man in front of him was a Federation Operative. And he had seen through his cover! Not only that, he was now being asked to help him in a secret operation. This was it! Forget his two year wait for promotion. If he helped out an operative, helped secure this data, saved lives, he would be out of here! If he could impress the Federation, he could get a job at the outer rim, taking out bandits and people smugglers. This could be his dream come true!

"Right, if what you're saying is true, and I decide to help you track this thief down..."

"...the Federation will be eternally grateful for your assistance. And if I'm telling a lie, you have me for trafficking, using a false identity, lying to a security official and anything else you care to slap on me."

To Barty, it sounded like a done deal. "OK. You have my assistance Mr Moss."

Higgs finally relaxed. Even *he* would admit this one had been a bit of a gamble, but if they couldn't finish this delivery, he wasn't sure how much longer he could fob off his creditors.

"Please call me Higgs in public. To maintain cover." Higgs tapped the side of his nose.

Barty smiled. "Absolutely Sir! So, what can I do to help?"

CHAPTER 13

The docking doors closed shut and the air pumps started filling the bay with oxygen as the sleek grey single person craft powered down. Inside, the figure in the black cloak sat motionless. He hacked the station security system in seconds and noted the impound and stowaway investigation in progress on The Lucky Duck. Both a useful and worrying development at the same time. He sent a secure transmission to his boss.

"Data card stolen again. Professional job. Loss risk too high at location. Take final action to secure?"

As the "Disembark notice" flashed up on his monitor from the control centre, he got his reply.

He allowed himself a smile as he read, "Confirmed. End this."

"Well Mr Flim, I think our store is looking particularly fine today."

"Indeed Mr Thinsy, I concur completely. Particularly fine."

"I have to say Mr Flim, that is a nicely arranged window display of writers' desk rearrangement tools."

"Why thank you Mr Thinsy, all the better for enticing plenty of procrastinating poets into the store."

"Ha ha! Indeed. I do hope we get plenty of customers today."

"Plenty customers."

"I have to say Mr Flim, that I am most happy with our latest store location. Bang in the middle trading routes with lots of monied people willing to spend."

"You make a fine point Mr Thinsy. One might say, a Lagrange point."

"Ha ha haaa! Oh my, Mr Flim, what a card you are. You always manage to brighten the day with some hilarious witticism."

"Ah, Mr Thinsy, it appears we have a customer."

"Oh, indeed so. A delightful genetically modified cat lady by the looks of it."

"Delightful."

"Furry."

"Indeed."

"I hope she finds what she's looking for."

"She should do. All our items are arranged carefully by product type in a standard snake like fashion round the shelves."

"Excellent. Although…"

"Do continue Mr Thinsy."

"I hope she isn't expecting an alphabetical arrangement."

"I do hope not."

"In which case, she may never find what she's looking for."

"I do hope not."

"Oh wait Mr Flim, she has picked up something. She is currently turning it over in her hands. She seems to be happy with it."

"That is good news. I hope she's happy with it."

"Why wouldn't she be? All our products are top quality goods."

"Top quality goods."

"Except the ones we got off the back of that Feldian transporter for 1000 credits."

"Except those ones."

"I hope that item isn't one of those ones."

Soap walked up to the counter.

"Hey guys, I'll take this thanks."

"Ah yes Madam, the 'Grabiculator TMA-42'. This little device mimics the gravitational conditions found down the back of a sofa and, when activated, will draw any small objects towards it from within fourteen centimetres. Most handy."

"Have you lost something small Madam?"

"Well *I* have no problems finding it, but a friend of mine keeps losing it. Every. Time."

"A very common situation I'm afraid, Madam."

"Just when he's on top of things, 'whoop!', he's lost it again."

"A most terrible shame. Twenty four credits please Madam."

"It's the frustration that gets me the most you know? For a brief moment it's 'Yes, yes!', then all of a sudden it's 'No, no!' while he goes and hunts around for it again."

"A sadly familiar tale I'm afraid, Madam. Here is your item, with your free gift for being such a lovely customer."

"Thanks, can't wait to try it out!"

"Neither can your friend, I'm sure. Good day Madam."

"Good day Madam."

"See ya."

Soap smiled at them and left the shop.

"I hope that item wasn't one of those ones."

"If it is then we're done for, it will break in minutes or it won't function properly to begin with."

"We're done for."

"Well she's left the store now. Purchase complete. Our product is out in the wild!"

"Oh dear, there goes our reputation Mr Flim, flung out of the airlock!"

"Flung indeed."

"She will be straight onto the DataNet to give us a scathing review."

"Oh dear…"

"Then she will go to a consumer rights lawyer and sue us for selling faulty items!"

"Oh dear…"

"Our reputation, orbiting the station amongst the rings of frozen faeces!"

"Faeces Mr Thinsy!"

"Our reputation, discarded along with the doo-doo detritus!"

"Faeces Mr Thinsy!"

"A stool satellite!"

"There's no other option, we have to abandon the store. Go on the run."

"Flee to a distant planet and start up the store from scratch."

"Go on the run."

"Somewhere where nobody knows us and our utterly ruined reputation. It's the only way Mr Flim!"

"I'll pack the cases, you grab the credits."

"Oh woe is me, why do all our ventures have to end in such calamity, why?!"

"It is our curse Mr Thinsy, our curse for selling such poor quality goods that customers easily find on our superbly arranged shelving displays."

"Wait… if we were to deliberately arrange our shelving displays such that customers can't find the poor quality goods…"

"Then they shall never be disappointed with a purchase they make!"

"And our reputation will be intact."

"Oh Mr Thinsy, what a cunning plan, why didn't we think of it before?"

"Because we're fools Mr Flim, utter incompetent fools, selling junk likely to kill our own customers."

"She's going to die!"

"Oh! The guilt grabs at my throat like a Jenovian whistling crocodile."

"She's going to die!"

"But not before we make our exit and escape the authorities. Two murderers by proxy fleeing justice!"

"To the space lanes Mr Thinsy, to a life on the run, no time for delay!"

"And don't forget our chudding lingerie this time."

$$\Leftarrow \bullet \Rightarrow$$

Outside the shop, Soap opened up the packet. The Grabiculator TMA-42 was a round metallic ball on the end of a folding plastic handle. Soap pointed it at a stray metal bolt lying on the ground. With a flick of a small switch, the bolt flew off the floor and stuck, upside down, to the surface of the ball.

"Works fine. Neat!"

CHAPTER 14

The shopping level was the busiest part of the station. It was comprised of two floors and arranged like a giant wheel. In the centre was a rotunda of retail units, arranged around the core of the station. Outside that, was a wide pedestrian aisle on the ground floor, while walkways on the floor above crossed over it like spokes. On the outside of the ring were more shops clustered between elevator access points to the other levels and various engineering and emergency passageways.

The retail stores upstairs were busy with duty free tourists, grabbing the low tax bargains on offer. The downstairs was mostly restaurants and food stores, and it had quietened down after the lunch rush. Patty's Pot Pie Parlour was situated on the outside ring of the lower floor. This was where Higgs had organised the meet and where Fred/Rick was already sitting on a seat outside, finishing off his meal.

Higgs and Barty were in a staff corridor further around the bend of the main thoroughfare. They were both watching Fred/Rick on their HUDs via the CCTV system.

"OK Barty, there's our guy."

"You sure that's him?"

"Absolutely. He didn't give me a physical description, too clever to do that, but he did give me a key code he said he would broadcast on an encrypted channel that only *I* know about. I can see the code, and it's pinging his location."

Barty shook his head in awe. "Wow, you techs amaze me."

"So, I'm going to approach him like an ancient lion, creep up on him through the long grass, stalk him with my words until I get from him what I need. Then I'm going to leap on him and eat... no I'm not going to do that bit, obviously. The analogy stops there. That's the bit where *you* and your men leap on him and... not eat him. Arrest him. Yes. You with me?"

"Every step of the way Sir."

"Good, good. Once I say the trigger phrase, that's when you subdue him. I grab the data card, and then he's all yours."

"Got it. I'll go join my men at the back of the restaurant across from him. I've got some others in place to block him off if he tries to run either way around the ring."

Higgs smiled. "You've got this well planned Barty. I'd expect nothing less from a man of your calibre."

"You can rely on me Sir. I'm going to just let you do your work and I'll be ready for you when you need me."

Barty saluted him and disappeared off down the corridor.

Higgs was able to relax for the first time since he went into Barty's office pod. "Oh God, I hope this works," he said to himself. "Have to get that data card. Have to get that data card…"

Higgs cracked his knuckles together and shook the tension out of his arms. He opened the door to the ring and confidently strode round towards the pie shop. Fred/Rick clocked him immediately and waved him over. Higgs sat down carefully and very sternly said "Hello."

The man opposite him wore a brown jacket with the hood down, revealing a small, square head topped with short blonde hair. He smiled, and deep curving lines bowed out across his cheeks.

"Hey man, the name's Fred/Rick, Swift Fred/Rick. Because I can be anywhere and gone in a matter of seconds, you get me?"

"I get you."

"No you don't."

"What, eh?"

"Because no-one gets me, I'm too fast! Ha-haa!" Fred/Rick slapped his hand on the table and laughed at his joke for what Higgs considered to be slightly too long.

Fred/Rick got his breath back. "Aw man, gets me every time."

"No you don't!" said Higgs, loudly.

Fred/Rick went silent and stared at him. "You what?"

"No you don't. Get me. I mean… get you. No-one gets you. Not even yourself. Because… you're too fast?"

Fred/Rick suddenly burst out laughing, much to Higgs' relief.

"That's it man, that's it!" He suddenly leaned forwards. "Hey, have you had the beef-like pie here? Delicious. Almost makes you wonder how much tastier a real beef could be. Not that there are any beefs around any more of course. I've seen the pictures of them though. Hard to believe they used to just wander around people's houses back on Earth. Weird things."

Higgs' reckoned he was stalling. He had to get him on to the topic of the job.

"Well Mr Fred/Rick, if that is indeed your name, and if it is then I might be, but only if you *are* Mr Fred/Rick, a certain Mr Moss whom you may have met on the SubNet, should such a thing exist, and if it did…"

Fred/Rick held up his hand.

"You're Turpentine Moss from the 'Things I Need To Be Found' forum. I get it."

"Well I *may* be…"

"And you're also my latest mark. Higgs Dittum. I just stole a data card from you and your companion Soap from on board your ship."

"She's not my companion! Why does everyone think..." Higgs stopped himself and just laughed nervously instead.

This wasn't going as expected. Fred/Rick had just admitted his theft without any prompting at all. Whilst fantastic, it didn't make him look good. He had to make sure Barty thought he was an agent until they could leave the station. If security suspected he wasn't an operative then they would never leave. How long was the prison term for impersonation a Federation official? He just needed to string this out a little longer.

"Oh, so you recognise me do you? I doubt it very much."

"But... it was you on the ship. I took the data card right from your pocket when you looked behind those boxes in your extremely empty hold."

"Ah, or *was* it?"

"Damn, this guy's good," whispered Barty to a colleague as they listened in to the conversation remotely. He and four other men were hidden out of sight in the kitchen of the Crunchy Fried Chicken-Like restaurant opposite Patty's Pot Pie Parlour, while they waited for their cue.

Fred/Rick grinned at the strange young man he had robbed not long ago. "Pretty sure it was, unless you floated here from Clarissa. In any case, I got you and your pilot's pictures from the client. I knew what you looked like from the off."

"Mmm, that's what *you* think Swift Fred/Rick."

"Anyhow, I knew it was you the moment you replied on that forum. It was too much of a coincidence man."

"Or *was* it?" said Higgs, smirking.

"Eh...yeh, yeh it was. I, like, steal the data card off you, then within the hour some random wants to meet face to face... oh, and just happens to be on Morley Station. Pfft! I mean, come on man, that's too much of a coincidence."

"Or *was* it?" said Higgs, nodding.

"Yeh. It was." said Fred/Rick, now slightly puzzled, but nodding in unison. "But it don't matter to Swift. Like I said in the ad I left you, I'm a thief. I have no loyalty once a job is finished. You want your data card back? Well, the moment I deliver it and the deal is sealed, you can hire me to lift it back off them."

Higgs decided he had done enough to keep his cover and gotten enough out of Fred/Rick to get him in custody. It was time to get his data card back.

"Ah, but the thing is Mr Swift, you're NOT LEAVING THIS STATION." Higgs nodded and looked over to the CFC-L restaurant.

"Yeah. I am. Don't take it personally Mr Dittum, I mean you're not the first person to approach me after a job for their stuff back, but I..."

"...am NOT LEAVING THIS STATION." said Higgs, slightly louder and more deliberately than before.

Nobody came rushing out of the chicken-like restaurant. Nobody blocked off the ring around them. Nobody knew the trigger phrase, because Higgs forgot to tell them what it was. The creeping realisation felt like cold water trickling down the back of his neck. He'd have to think of some other way to end this. Higgs had to get Barty and his men out here now, but without letting on to Swift. He had to be subtle with this.

"So, are you going to HELP ME or not? Mr Fred/Rick. HELP ME?"

"Yeh. Like I said, once the package is delivered, get in contact and I'm all yours."

Higgs glanced over at the restaurant. "Sooo... you *are* going to HELP ME?"

Fred/Rick nodded carefully. "Yeh, yeh. That's what I said."

"OK. Great. You're going to HELP. ME. Sooo... I can't help but notice your accent there Mr Swift. Are you RUSH IN?"

In the back of the CFC-L, Barty looked around at the armed men crouched behind the deep fat fryer. "Ah, you see what he's doing guys? He's trying to get him at ease, get to know him personally so he lets his guard down. You listen men, this is a professional at work here."

Fred/Rick sat back in his chair. "No, my ancestors were Earth-German actually, though I'm surprised you can pick up any accent at all. Everybody speaks mixed galactic now."

Higgs kept twisting his eyes over to the restaurant but there was no sign of movement.

"So you're not going to STOP. THIEF?"

"Heck no! My whole family were thieves. I was taught from a young age how to pickpocket, scam and break and enter without so much of a whisper of me left behind. It runs in the blood. I say you gotta do what you were born to do. No point fighting it to keep other people or the police happy. Use your skills. It's the way it is."

"Sooo... would you say you are READY FOR ACTION?"

"Ey?"

"For the job. The data card."

"You haven't hired me yet. And you can't until I deliver it. That's not how I work. Look Mr Dittum, it's been great to speak to you, but I have a deadline to meet here. You know how to contact me, so be in touch!"

Fred/Rick stood up suddenly and started to walk away. Higgs jumped up in panic.

"ATTACK! ATTACK!" he said, leaping up and down.

Fred/Rick looked around, confused. "What?"

Barty smiled and nodded to his men. "Ah, confusion. Great tactic. Confuse the enemy so they are disorientated and vulnerable."

"This guy's good," said the guard crouched next to him.

"Told you. A master at work. OK. Get ready, I think our time's coming up."

Higgs stared open mouthed into the restaurant. The girl behind the counter shrugged at him as she looked down at the men hiding by her legs.

Fred/Rick was looking all around now, scanning every person he saw. "What is this?"

"A... A... A TACK! On the floor. I thought I saw ATTACK... on the floor... didn't want you stepping on it."

Nothing happened. Defeated, Higgs dropped his head into his hands. "Did it once when I was a kid and it *really* hurt..."

"See, he's bonding with him on an emotional level now. Finding a connection between them he can use to extract..."

"BARTY, FOR THE LOVE OF GOD COME AND GET THIS GUY NOW!"

"...information and... oh... right, GO GO GO!"

By the time station security had burst out of the restaurant doors, Fred/Rick was already out of sight.

CHAPTER 15

The last thing Higgs saw was Fred/Rick disappearing round the bend.

The next thing Higgs saw was Fred/Rick reappearing round the bend.

"There he is Barty, stop him!"

Barty and his men formed a line, pointing their guns at the thief.

"Right, stowaway, you stop right there or you'll discover why we have a reputation as the hardest security staff this side of the galaxy."

Fred/Rick just shook his head as he ran at them. "Trust me, I'm running from worse," he shouted as he suddenly veered to one side, leapt onto a table and vaulted over the line.

"Hey! Nobody does that to a Morley Station officer!"

Barty and his men began to give chase as Higgs mulled over his words, "Running from worse?"

As he looked back down the ring, four very angry Grey Dragons appeared.

"Oh no... eyes front Barty!"

Barty spun round. "Oi! How many times do I have to tell you guys? You lot are banned from this station until you pay for that automatic toilet you broke..."

The Dragons pulled out extending blades and small curved metal objects that created umbrella-like energy shields at the flick of a switch.

"Men, behind us! Weapons free!"

Higgs dodged round them as the security line turned and started firing. The Dragons ducked behind tables as energy blasts exploded around them. One caught one on his energy shield and knocked it out of his hand. The glasses Dragon pressed a button on the side of his blade handle and small section of blade fired off and buried itself in the leg of one of Barty's men.

"Get to cover!" shouted Barty as energy blasts and blade projectiles sparked off the walls and floor.

Higgs tried to block out the chaos behind him as he saw the back of Fred/Rick disappearing the other way round the ring as terrified onlookers dropped to the floor.

"Not this time you don't!" he said and ran after him.

⇐•⇒

Soap was walking out of the Fresh Enough store with a few more tins of Chewna-Chunx when she heard the gunfire from the other side of the ring.

"Oop, sounds like it's on."

She dropped the bag and jogged round the outside of the top floor towards the noise, as people ran for their lives in the opposite direction. It was then she spotted a tall figure in a long black coat in front of her, slowly walking through the flow of panicked shoppers. She could smell nothing about him at all. This guy was heavily genetically modified.

"Well, well Mr Fred/Rick, let's see where *you're* going," she said, following him.

Higgs was no athlete, and he knew that any attempt at chasing anyone was never going to end as intended, but this was his livelihood getting away. This was his job going down the VacuFlush. He had to at least make it look convincing so he could claim the danger fee from the client. Much to his surprise, he didn't have to run for long to catch up with Fred/Rick. He was standing still in the middle of the ring.

"A-ha! I have you now mister master thief!"

Fred/Rick spun round. "Who the hell have you scoofed off man?" he screamed, then ran sideways through the staff doors into the corridor where Higgs had gone over the plan with Barty.

Just in front of Higgs now stood six muscular thugs, bald but for a single line of hair going diagonally from one ear over the top of their heads. The largest one pointed at Higgs. "Him!" he said as they drew their guns.

"Chud!" Higgs darted after Fred/Rick as he heard heavy feet slamming into the floor behind him.

Fred/Rick ran through a side door into the kitchen of a restaurant. Higgs quickly followed, energy blasts ripping chunks out of the walls around him.

"What have you got me into?" cried Fred/Rick as he pushed a chef out of the way and jumped through a connecting door into the next restaurant.

Higgs scrambled after him, hopping over fallen woks and boxes. "You think I planned *this*?"

The door behind him crashed open and six huge men tried to force their way through it simultaneously, until they realised they had to go through one at a time.

"I don't care what you planned, but I'm gettin' outta it now!"

"I don't suppose you've got an escape plan then?"

"But you just did."

"What? This is not helping!"

Fred/Rick disappeared out the front of the kitchen and leapt over the counter. Diners, already hiding under their tables from the sound of gunfire, screamed as he ran past them. He appeared just behind the Grey Dragons, the air filled with the burning rock stench of energy weapons.

"Perfect," he thought to himself. He would use the chaos to lose himself amongst the other shoppers and head back to the docking ring for his ride home. Unfortunately, the fleeing shoppers parted around another line of security staff heading towards the fighting.

"Oh foob..." he said, and ran straight across into the restaurant opposite instead.

⇐•⇒

On the walkway above, the tall cloaked figure had been watching the to-ing and fro-ing below. His eyes followed Fred/Rick into the restaurant and he quickly ducked into the clothes shop above it.

Soap, hidden in a doorway some distance away, watched him go.

"Yep, you're definitely the guy I'm looking for," she said to herself as she followed him into the shop.

⇐•⇒

Higgs, meanwhile, had emerged from the kitchen, After an unsuccessful attempt to vault over the counter, that ended with his shins cracking on the edge of the worktop, he feebly lifted the service flap and hobbled through the small half door below it.

Outside the restaurant he found himself between the Dragons and a line of security staff approaching with their guns up. There was no sign of Fred/Rick.

"Chud!" he shouted, making the nearest Dragon turn round and spot him. He gulped as he recognised the glasses Dragon.

Higgs waved, "Oh, hi there," and vanished back into the restaurant.

In seconds the Dragons broke cover and converged on the doorway.

"They're running scared! We've got them guys, come on!" cried Barty as he led the chase.

Higgs ran back into the kitchen as the chef was just getting back off the floor.

"Not you again!"

"Worse!"

The six thugs burst through the side door just as the four Grey Dragons dived in from the front. The two groups of men studied each other in silence for a moment, then leapt towards each other, fists, blades and guns blasting.

⇐•⇒

Swift Fred/Rick excused himself to the kitchen staff as he walked past them towards the back of the shop. He just needed to get to the service corridor then he would have the run of the station back to the docking ring. Bypass security, hack control of The Lucky Duck back from the tower and he would be out of here.

Sometimes a job would go polar like this, but he tried to prevent it by being clever. He was a sneak thief after all. Guns and knives were not his thing. Sneak, sneak. Quickly and quietly. Deliver and collect. And you never know, if that Higgs guy was still alive he might get that "revenge thievery" job after all. "Heh, am I extraordinary or what?" He said, smiling to himself as he pushed open the back door.

In front of him stood a tall thin figure dressed in black. He wore a mask over the lower half of his face and his eyes were covered, or perhaps replaced, with dark goggles that stared directly at him.

"Man, I'm beginning to think this job is not worth the hassle."

Higgs was sprawled on the floor next to the chef, who had decided it was the safest place to be after all, as his kitchen was ripped to pieces around him.

"Rear exit?"

The chef pointed with a trembling arm to a small office.

"Lovely."

One of the thugs slid over the table top, before hitting the floor next to them with a heavy thud, plates and utensils clattering to the floor.

"I'm going now," said Higgs. He scrambled to his feet and, keeping low, crept round to the office and made his exit out the back.

The glasses Dragon had spotted him go. As one of the thugs tried to grapple him, he punched him in the neck. The man dropped to the floor. The Dragon ordered his men to tidy up here as he stepped over the cowering chef and went through to the office.

The lead thug had also spotted him go. As one of the Dragons ran at him, he ripped an entire wall unit from its fastenings and threw it at him. The Dragon, plus unit, bounced away from him. He knew his men would take care of business here as he stepped over the still cowering chef and went through to the office.

⇐•⇒

"There you are!"

The tall figure, who had just emerged from the back door of the restaurant, stared at Soap.

"So, you gonna give me that data card Mr Fred/Rick, or am I gonna have to grab it from ya?"

The figure gave a quiet chuckle.

"Oh, right. You think I'm... what... not a match for you Mister? Is that it? Think little kitty-cat me couldn't take on a big cyborg like you?"

The figure stopped chuckling. With a flick of his arms, long blades shot out above his wrists.

"Oh sorry, you're just one of the chefs. For a moment I thought you were actually a bad-ass or something."

Soap flexed her fingers and her claws popped out. With a snarl she ran at him.

He swung his blades at her but she ducked underneath, slid onto her bottom and kicked her legs into his stomach.

The back door was ripped of its hinges as the man hit it and tumbled into the kitchen. He came to a halt as he slammed into a metal unit.

Soap stood in the doorway, holding the data card in her fingers. "So, we equal now or what?"

The man grimaced, got to his feet and leapt at her.

Higgs panted as he fell out of the gift shop, clutching onto a "Wanna dock with me?" Morley Station branded t-shirt. There was a commotion behind him and he could see two figures half running, half trying to punch each other, and getting closer.

This wasn't good. His lungs were already burning and his legs shook as he picked himself up and ran across the walkway to the outer edge of the ring. He had thought that getting to the upper level might shake them off, but they were still on him. Suddenly, Soap appeared from the clothes shop in front of him.

"Higgs, you're still alive!"

"Momentarily!"

She grabbed his arm and pulled him along after her. The lead Dragon and the lead thug almost collided with the tall coated figure as he exited the shop, before they all untangled their legs and gave chase.

Soap spotted the sign for 'Escape Pods' down an exit to the right.

"Hey, I've got an idea!" said Soap, grabbing Higgs by his top and hurling him down the walkway past the exit. She stopped and turned to face the chasing trio.

"You want the data card? Then you want *me*!"

She ducked down the side exit and the three men followed her. It led to a small brightly lit open area with coloured lines on the floor leading to a row of closed doors, each one an escape pod entrance.

The three men found her standing in front of the doors facing them, hands on hips. "So, you wanna all have a go at me at once and risk losing the data card to someone else, or do you wanna work it out now, you know, between yourselves, who gets it?"

The three men decided to work it out between themselves first.

As Higgs sat on the ground, slowly getting his breath back, he noticed the sounds of gunfire had stopped. He got to his feet and looked over the walkway railing to see Barty and most of his men still alive below them.

"Everything under control down there officer?"

Barty saluted. "All taken care of Sir. Did you find your thief?"

"Yeah. He's... uh, taken care of too. I think." Higgs could hear the sounds of fighting from near the escape pods. "But my colleague could do with some of your firepower up here."

"Right away Sir!" Barty barked orders at his men and they quickly made for the nearest stairwell.

Higgs puffed the air out of his chest and shook his legs. "I hope I never have to run like that ever again," he said as he patted his chest.

As he patted his chest, he felt something small and hard in his breast pocket. He pulled out the data card.

"How did this even...?"

There was a scream from near the escape pods.

"Soap! Soap, it's OK, you can stop fighting them!"

Higgs ran down the exit tunnel and emerged into the pod waiting area.

"Hey, Soap, it's OK. I've got the data card, I've no idea where it came from though..."

On the floor lay two men. One muscular thug in combats and one grey skinned suited Dragon wearing VR glasses.

Soap was lying against the wall, clutching her stomach, her shirt stained red with blood. Standing over her was a tall thin figure in a long dark coat. He was holding a data card in his fingers. He looked at Higgs, then at the data card *he* was holding.

"OK, now this is confusing."

In three deft strides the figure was in front of Higgs and had taken his card too. Higgs gazed into the dark circles of the man's goggles, but couldn't make out any eyes behind them.

"I guess it's got to be one of them, right? And you've got two now. Talk about a bonus... yeah?"

There was a noise of slicing metal as a long blade, smeared with blood, slid out from inside the man's arm.

"I'll throw in some packets of fresh apple if you don't kill me?"

"Stop thief!"

Behind Higgs, a line of tooled up and very, very angry security guards took aim at the figure.

With a glance the man bolted for the pods. With a flick of his HUD he tripped the emergency system, starting a loud wailing alarm and unlocking the pod doors.

Soap pushed herself up to her feet and pulled something out of her thigh pocket. "Knew he'd do that."

As the man dived into a pod and triggered the eject sequence, Soap flicked the switch on the Grabiculator and threw it towards the pod. There was a buzzing noise and two data cards flew threw the gap in the closing doors. The doors slammed shut and the Grabiculator bounced off it, both cards stuck firmly to its physics warping surface.

As the eject sequence locked in, and the pod systems disconnected from the station systems for safety, the figure felt something was missing. He looked through the glass in the doors to see Soap swinging the end of the Grabiculator around outside with the two cards on the end of it.

"Hey Mister! You lost something? You looking for something? You looking for something small? I bet you are. I bet you're looking for something really small. Something really small like a data card, aren't you Mister? You looking for a data card Mister? I bet you are."

The man in the pod slammed his hands against the glass of the door.

"You OK in there Mister? You meant to be in there? You trapped in there? Caged? Caught? I don't think you're meant to be in there. You stuck in there Mister? Unable to get out? Does that annoy you? Upset you? Make you look like a fool? Do you feel like a fool? Like everyone thinks you're a fool? I bet you feel like a fool. Stuck in there?"

The figure stood back from the door, arms straight down by his sides, fists tight and shaking.

"Bet you wish you'd never gone in there now. Bet you wish you were somewhere else instead. Somewhere not stuck inside there. Like a fool. Don't you Mister? Bye!"

A bulkhead door slid into place between the station and the pod and there was a loud clunking noise as the pod was safely jettisoned.

Higgs appeared at Soap's shoulder. "You got the data card? Cards?"

"Yep. I also got a screw and eighty grams of pocket lint."

"So how...?"

"Flim & Thinsy had a special deal on: buy any item and get a free, blank data card. No-one uses them any more so I guess they had a pile to get rid of."

"That was brilliant. You slip me the real data card for safety and get them chasing you for the dud. Sorry I almost got the real one stolen again."

"To be honest, I've no idea which one is ours any more. Kind of lost track around the part where I fled for my life."

"You OK by the way?" Higgs looked down at Soap's bloody stomach.

"Yeah, just a flesh wound. That Swift Fred/Rick guy is *very* swift."

"That wasn't Swift Fred/Rick."

"What?"

"Yeah, I've no idea where *he's* gone. But this..." Higgs plucked one of the data cards from the end of the Grabiculator "is definitely the card we're after. So, who cares?" he shrugged.

"Well who was *that* guy then?" Soap thumbed at the bulkhead.

"Someone tumbling into the deepest reaches of space forever."

"Actually, those pods are programmed to head for the nearest safe landing pad." Barty was standing next to them, holding a four foot long pulse rifle, its butt jammed into his hip. "Nearest one to here is back on Clarissa. I'll radio ahead and warn Williams City Spaceport. They'll make sure he gets a full military welcome!" He grinned.

"Nice work Barty." Higgs patted him on his shoulder.

"I'll get medical to check over your colleague here."

"No really, I'm fine…"

Barty held up his hand. "It's the least we can do before we set you back on your way." He nodded at them both and strode away. "Men, secure the shopping ring, and get the medics up here. I want Mr Mo… er, Dittum's ship unlocked for take-off and these guys' ships," he pointed at the two bodies on the floor, "impounded immediately, full checks and alert the Fed Crime Bureau. And for the love of foob someone turn off that chudding alarm!"

CHAPTER 16

With her skin wound sealed, Soap was in the cockpit preparing for take off. Higgs and Barty stood at the gate to the landing bay. Since the incident, the station had been a hive of activity. Security staff were busy running back and forth, escorting engineers and medics to where they were needed. Despite the chaos, there appeared to be a renewed sense of purpose about the station and Higgs could only smile as Barty scratched at a bandage on his face.

"… and as soon as our engineers force their way inside their ships, I'll pass on any information we find on these guys. Some real dangerous people were after that data: Grey Dragons, The Beat Mob, that cyborg fella, not to mention Swift Fred/Rick, wherever the hell *he's* gotten to."

"Don't worry, he can't have gone far. In any case, the data is secure, that's all that matters right now. And I'm sure you'll find something we can use to track his employer."

"Oh we will. Don't you worry Mr Moss. He's still on this station somewhere. It's only a matter of time."

Barty excused himself for a moment to point two guards in the direction of the weapons room.

"I see you're all tooled up now?"

"Well, what good is it confiscating all these guns if you can't use them at your own discretion now and again?"

"You know Barty, I've spoken to Alpha Command about your situation..."

"Did you tell them what I've done for you? About helping your mission?"

"I did. They are incredibly impressed with your flexibility and resourcefulness. Not so impressed with *my* work, but that's a disciplinary I will have to deal with when I get back."

Barty looked horrified. "But that wasn't your fault, he was a master criminal!"

"It doesn't matter. That data was my responsibility and mine alone. I take the fall for that one. Just as your service has been recognised and will be rewarded."

"Rewarded?" said Barty, almost hopping on the spot with delight.

"Command has decided to grant you 'Morley Station Special Operative' status."

Barty looked confused. "What... what does that mean? I had always hoped to go after bandits on the outer rim. They're on the news every day, a scourge on the colonies out there. With these guns..."

Higgs put a hand on his shoulder and whispered. "Trust me, we have that situation well in hand. Half of them are our people, just biding their time, waiting for the right moment." Then he gave Barty a wink.

"Really? Wow. I see, so what do I need to do here?"

"Use these guns to keep your station secure. We need you for intel gathering. No-one else is so well placed in this sector to monitor the movements of smugglers. Command needs you to carry on as normal, as if nothing has changed. But you will be secretly providing us data on all shipments you deem suspicious. You know your job. You have the skills. You know what to do."

Barty smiled. That was the phrase from Space Unit Alpha. He couldn't believe they actually used the same one in real life.

"You know, I always knew I was destined for more than sitting on this space station for months on end. And it turns out I was! We do what we do best."

Higgs smiled back. "We do what we do best. Oh and, as an extra bonus, while I'm still on operational duty for our undercover delivery company, anything you need delivered, anywhere, any time."

"Anything?"

"Anything at all. First one's free, but I will have to charge you after that. To maintain cover you know. It would look a bit suspicious to have too many free deliveries on the books."

"No, no, I understand completely. And in return, you will have free passage through here. Any time you need, no boardings or checks."

"Really?"

"Oh yes. Barty will take care of it. It's the least I can do as a fellow operative!"

They shook hands, then Higgs strode off through the docking gate out of sight as Barty watched on.

"Damn. That's one hell of a guy."

An engineer removed the broken door from the kitchen and laid it on a large trolley at the back of the restaurant. It would be a while before they replaced it.

Inside the kitchen, the head chef shouted at his staff to help the waiters and get tidying out front.

"The ring may be closed but we need to be ready for when it's reopened. No slacking!"

It would be a while before they would have any customers back in.

As the staff gathered mops and buckets, grumbling to themselves, the body of Swift Fred/Rick slowly chilled inside the large chest freezer by the back door. It would be a while before anyone found him.

CHAPTER 17

"And we're finally here!" grinned Soap as The Lucky Duck finished its descent through the atmosphere and followed a gentle arc until it was travelling parallel to the surface of the planet.

Scylla was exceptionally barren; a small, radiation scoured ball of rock. But it had two things going for it. Firstly, it was perfectly positioned in the middle of major transport and trade routes through the sector. Secondly, it was highly geothermically active, with tens of thousands of huge natural lava tubes that disappeared miles into the crust. It was inside one of these tubes that Varda City One was built.

Soap had stopped the ship and was hovering between two rows of guiding lights that led to the edge of the hole. The lights were currently all red as they waited for landing confirmation.

Higgs had been rooting under the cockpit dashboard for something, but was now straining up out of his seat.

"Can't see..."

Soap pressed a button on the dashboard and a screen near Higgs flicked from technical data to a camera view of the surface beneath them.

"We have an under camera? Neat!"

Moments later, the control tower gave Soap the landing instructions and the lights turned amber. She gently brought the ship over the edge of the tube and started to descend along the flight path on her navigation screen, while Higgs stared, goggle-eyed, at the view of the city below.

While the surface baked in the nearby sun's radiation, the tube was protected by miles of rock. Light collectors fixed around the lip of the tube allowed the city to control its climate and have an artificial day/night cycle, while power lines that went deep down into the tube below the city provided far more energy than it could ever need. It was also naturally nice and warm down there which, to the city engineers' dismay, contributed more to the house prices than all their work combined. The residential property was dug into the rock around the outer rim of the tube, safe from any direct radiation bursts, meaning the main bulk of the city inside the tube itself were commercial and farming areas.

The city was a massive spider's web of walkways and bridges spanning a chasm so deep, that all the Health & Safety inspectors must have thrown themselves into it in defeat the moment they arrived. Huge districts of skyscrapers hung over empty space, subsequent generations of architects enjoying making each new building's design seem ever more terrifyingly perilous. Large parks and plazas hovered in thin air with the thinnest of supports connecting them to the outer edge and the central Spire, the mile high building containing all the city's administration and services. At the top of the Spire was the Spaceport, sat on it like a giant flower that stretched to the outer edges of the tube. Each petal was a terminal and all the ships slowly dropping and rising from it were tiny worker bees, coming and going with the city's nectar. As they dropped, two huge Tosen Transport ships, dark blue with rims of blinking yellow lights, rose up past them. Higgs eyed them enviously.

"One day we'll have a fleet of ships that big Soap. One day."

Then he went back to rummaging in the drawers and shelves around his feet.

"Whatcha after?"

"I bought a nanotracker a while ago. Was going to test it out on our shipments in case they went missing or got stolen. Then we never got any shipments. Thought I would pop it in the data card. Just in case we lose it again."

"Why don'tcha use the Grabiculator? It'll find it in no time."

Higgs face lit up. "Oh yeah." He unbuckled himself and disappeared into Soap's quarters.

Varda City One was the first city built in the tubes of Scylla and now there were eight others. There had been a tenth city, but a somewhat hasty geological survey, before the Federation claimed control and changed the regulations, meant that the city builders hadn't fully certified that the tube they were building in was inactive. It wasn't, and Varda City Ten gained the unenviable reputation of being the first city in orbit, before it quickly left orbit and disappeared into extrasolar space.

Higgs returned with the Grabiculator, flicked it on and swept over the shelves and corners of the cockpit. While he did this, Soap followed the flight path to the Economy landing area and parked in the marked bay. It meant a walk to the terminal, but saved them a few credits. As she powered down the engines and waited for the control tower to lock their flight systems, a small fleet of service robots and a large van approached them.

"Got it!" shouted Higgs, and pulled the Grabiculator out of a small drawer next to the emergency medical kit on the wall. He picked a tiny black dot off it and sat down next to her as he took the data card from his pocket.

"You know, we've been here before, but we've never been down into the city itself," said Higgs. "Apparently they've these gardens so large they have their own micro climate. They get tiny clouds down there!"

"The place is pretty tightly regulated though, so we'd best try and stay out of trouble. No more jumping off trains or hacking auto-drives OK?"

Higgs saluted, "Yessir! Oop…" and flung the tiny dot somewhere over his shoulder.

"Seriously, they have a really strict AI that controls everything, keeps order. One of the guys on my engineering course was born here and he told me it's a really nice place to live, provided you just agree with everything,"

"Sounds like a truly modern Utopia. In any case, I can agree with things," nodded Higgs, sweeping the Grabiculator across the floor, "I'm pretty good at agreeing with things. In fact, I'm doing it now. Dead easy."

The van turned sideways on and stopped in front of their ship as the robots disappeared from their view underneath them.

"Got it! Again. Right. Priority one, above anything else: get the data card to the customer. As soon as we're outside the restricted areas of the Spire, we'll get in contact and ask for delivery coordinates. Then we'll drop it off, get some food and hopefully people will stop trying to kill us!"

"Just what is it about the data on that thing that makes it so valuable anyway?"

Higgs shook his head. "I really don't know. I've been over it dozens of times and it's just a load of old family photos, scans of letters and a video of some kids playing. I don't get why it's so important. But, I guess I don't have to. I just have to deliver it and get paid before I die."

"Who needs payment when you've got your life, right?"

Higgs made a face. "From a strictly business perspective, that doesn't *really* work, but I see your point. Don't worry Soap, I've got a feeling things are going to pick up for us."

The side of the van rolled up and a dozen helmeted soldiers in grey and red armour jumped out, formed a line and pointed their weapons towards the cockpit window. Their internal speakers crackled into life as the tower took control of their ship.

"COME OUT WITH YOUR HANDS UP! WE APOLOGISE FOR THE INCONVENIENCE YOU HAVE CAUSED YOURSELF. YOU KNOW WHAT YOU SHOULDN'T HAVE DONE."

Higgs sighed. "I'll never get to see those clouds."

CHAPTER 18

The door to the office of the Head of Customs beeped and slid open as a junior official in his red and grey uniform walked in.

"Sir, those two smugglers are ready for interrogation in room four. "

"Thank you Bevans," said the young woman sat behind the desk. She didn't look up from her data tablet.

"Oh and, I was going to leave this to the surface workers, but..."

The head of jet black hair still didn't look up.

"...CLARA has informed us that, about ten minutes ago, an escape pod crashed on the surface, four kilometres from the edge of the tube."

Tara Brissoles finally looked up from her holoscreen.

"An escape pod? Which ship?"

"Not a ship, Sir. It appears to be from Morley Station."

Tara stood up slowly and leant her knuckles on the edge of her desk.

"Morley? That's impossible!" Her face changed from confusion to resignation. "Well, it's maximum solar activity this month, so if there *was* anyone on board they will be fried by radiation by now. Fried like a pair of hot, horny lovers in a sauna. How many were on board?"

"That's the other thing, CLARA couldn't access its systems to get any flight data, she was firewalled out. Then it just went dead when it hit."

Tara rubbed her chin. "Very suspicious if you ask me. OK, get in touch with Morley, find out what the hell is going on with that chudhole and send a robot up to the surface to inspect. I'm not risking any men on another one of their tech failures. I remember the last time that happened: they programmed a refuse ship with the wrong coordinates and it ended up crashing into landing pad six. That place needs a good boot up the tont if you ask me."

"Right away Sir."

The officer left and Tara did some stretches in the middle of the office before flicking her long black hair over her shoulders and leaving the room. As she walked down the corridor to the interrogation room there was a chiming noise.

bing dong
"WELCOME TO VARDA CITY ONE CUSTOMS HOLDING FACILITY. IF YOU ARE HERE, YOU SHOULD NOT HAVE DONE THAT."

Tara nodded in agreement with the announcement as she reached the door. The CLARA AI scanned her face as she approached and unlocked it for her.

Inside sat a man with tall hair and a feline woman, both strapped securely to holding chairs on the opposite side of a table. Already in the room was a senior officer, reading their details from a central holoscreen. As Tara came in, he stood up and saluted.

"Sir!"

"Kim." She nodded and he sat down again. Tara sat in the other chair and looked at her suspects.

She said, "Recording on," and there was a quiet beep. "I hope you are finding the accommodation to your liking?"

Soap strained forwards. "You munting think...?"

"No we're both fine, aren't we Soap? Yes?"

Soap gave him a look of horror.

"Yeah, really comfortable facility you have here Miss...?"

"Brissoles. Head of Customs, Varda City One."

"Ah, perfect. Just the person I wanted to talk to."

"Except you will be doing no talking here. CLARA?"

"WE RESERVE THE RIGHT TO SHUT YOU UP BECAUSE WE CARE ABOUT YOUR SAFETY," boomed a sharp voice from somewhere in the room. Higgs and Soap twisted their heads around, but couldn't find the source.

Tara laughed. "That's CLARA. She is the AI that runs Varda City One for the safety of *all* of us. Including those who have done wrong. Thanks CLARA."

"YOU ARE WELCOME OFFICER BRISSOLES."

"But we haven't done wrong! Unless I missed out a field in that rather complicated online landing permission form..."

"It's not complicated!" interrupted an obviously irritated Officer Kim, "It's thorough!"

"It's a thorough pain in the tont."

Kim clenched his fists and looked ready to launch himself across the table at Higgs until Tara held up her hands.

"Gentlemen, please! Any feedback you have on the form can be given directly to Officer Kim, as he is in charge of our self-service docking facilities."

"Really? Well, you keep using "it's" when it should be "its" and there's a glaring typo on page four..."

"OUR MISTAKES SHOW WE ARE FALLIBLE. YOUR MISTAKES THREATEN THE EXISTENCE OF ORDER."

"Indeed CLARA. You can give feedback later. First of all we need to go over some basics. You are Higgs Dittum are you not? The owner of Higgs & Soap: Galaxy Delivery?"

"Yes."

"And you are Soap Hathaway-Jones, flight engineer and pilot?"

"And business partner!"

Tara tapped at her data tablet. "Ah, so you will be part liable too…"

Soap cursed quietly to herself.

"Which means you both own The Lucky Duck, the Class-A2 transport with ID LKE-D00K currently sat on Economy landing pad sixteen?"

They both nodded.

"Great. Now I would like to discuss the contraband you have brought to this city. Right this very moment we have men hunting, fingering every nook and cranny of your ship like a hot lover discovering their partner's body. We will find your hiding place eventually, but if you want quick relief, just tell me now where your goods are stashed."

Soap's ears pricked up. "But we aren't carrying any contraband!"

"Not for lack of trying," muttered Higgs.

"I'm sorry, could you speak up for the recording…"

"I said we wouldn't know where to buy it. Contraband that is. We're just honest delivery people Ms Brissoles."

"Hmm. So if you're not carrying any contraband, then how come I got an anonymous communication from someone in this city telling me otherwise?"

Higgs thought for a moment. "Prank call? Most likely another delivery firm. It's a cutthroat business sometimes, and some companies are not above doing a little 'dirty work' to discredit their competitors."

"Of course, Mr Dittum. You know, it may not be obvious to you what you have brought in that's contraband. We have some of the strictest customs controls here in Varda City One."

"WE STOP YOU ENJOYING YOURSELF IN CASE YOU HURT YOURSELF. THAT IS HOW MUCH WE CARE."

"Exactly CLARA. But we do like to give people one chance to go through our list of contraband items to make sure they aren't breaking the law. And that one chance happens before you get here. It's too late now."

"IF YOU DO NOT KNOW WHAT YOU DID WRONG, YOU SOON WILL. FOR A VERY LONG TIME."

"Absolutely CLARA."

Higgs started shaking in the chair as Soap stared down at the floor.

"Can... can I just check that all our belongings are secure?" asked Higgs.

"Yeah, like the lack of stuff in our cargo hold..."

"The data card from my breast pocket..."

"My furball collection..."

"The data card from my breast pocket..."

"WE CARE ABOUT YOUR POSSESSIONS BECAUSE YOU WILL NEVER SEE THEM AGAIN."

"What, CLARA?" cried Higgs and Soap in unison.

"I'm afraid that because you're under investigation, all your goods are now property of the Varda City One Customs."

Higgs leaned his head over to Soap. "Well, at least it's secure." He spoke up to the room: "Is it secure CLARA?"

"AS SECURE AS YOUR CONTINUED INCARCERATION IN THIS ROOM."

"Perfect, thanks CLARA! Well I don't know about you Soap, but that's a weight off *my* mind."

Soap quietly fumed, ears pinned back. "I can't believe I'm going to prison for *not* smuggling. How's that for irony."

Higgs spotted the frown on Tara's face. "Yep, *not* smuggling. That's what we do. We not... don't smuggle. Not. Just normal deliveries."

There was a beep from the holoscreen and a message titled "Suspects 0451, goods inspection complete. One (1) contraband item found."

"Oh dear," said Kim. "Looks like you're going to be spending a lot more of your time filling out forms," he grinned.

Tara opened the message on the screen. "Looks like you were carrying a physics alteration device. Something called a Grabiculator TMA-42?"

"That's contraband?" said Soap.

"My dear, our city is suspended over a twelve mile deep lava tube. The warmth from below breezes past you on the walkways like a hot lover disappearing under your duvet. Any item than can alter or affect the laws of physics could send the entire city plummeting into the core of the planet. Hardly ideal, I'm sure you would agree?"

"But it only picks up tiny objects..."

"ANY item."

"THIS CITY ONLY SURVIVES BECAUSE WE ARE SO HARD ON YOU."

Tara gestured to the air. "See?"

"Is nanotech banned too?" asked Higgs.

"Absolutely! We have the highest certified non-nano plant and human population in the galaxy and we intend to keep it that way. Why? Did you bring any?"

"No, no... just a general question..." muttered Higgs, as Kim hurriedly scanned over the report.

"A full nanotech marker sweep was done, and none were found on their ship or their person, Sir."

"Oh... dear... good. Yes, just as I told you. No nanotech," said Higgs, as he realised the data card was not secured with the other items.

Tara took all this in carefully, and turned to the young man sat next to her. "OK, Officer Kim, you can leave. I think we have everything we need. I'll take it from here."

The man leapt to his feet, saluted with a "Sir!" and briskly left the room.

Tara stood up, eyeing the two suspects in front of her. They fixed her stare right back, following her as she paced back and forth, working out what to say next. In the end, she just gave them a massive grin.

"Recording off."

beep

"Smugglers! Actual smugglers. I can't believe I'd ever lay eyes on some. Oh wow, I'm so excited!"

Tara was jumping up and down on the spot, clutching her arms to her chest. She suddenly sat down, leaning right across the table.

"You ever smuggled people? Are you the really, really bad ones I hear about? Like... *really* hurt people? I mean... badly?"

She urgently looked back and forth between Higgs and Soap. They gave each other a slightly puzzled look.

"You know like, kill people? Murder them? To silence them?"

"We... have hurt people. Yes."

"I knew it!" Tara clapped her hands.

"Mostly accidentally mind you."

"I hit a radio tower once when I was learning to fly..."

"And there was that time I bumped into this guy... I think I elbowed him in the ribs."

"You must have had some desperate chases from the law though?"

Soap nodded. "Oh heck yes, this one gets us into so much trouble I always end up being the one to pull his tont out of the fire."

"She *is* an ace pilot. The stories I could tell..."

"And you will. You will. You'll tell me everything about your adventures! This is brilliant."

"Er, can I ask, why are you so big on smugglers?" asked Higgs. "I thought you'd be glad to not have to deal with any?"

Tara plopped herself back in the chair and puffed out her cheeks. "None of them ever come here! It's sooo boring. The rules here are so strict, punishments so harsh and, if you will let me be somewhat immodest for a moment, we have the best customs department in the galaxy, that nobody dares try! Oh how I have longed to meet some actual, real, up-to-space smugglers! Wow, you guys are ace!"

For the first time in a while, Soap allowed herself a smile. "So you *want* to meet dangerous smugglers?"

"Why do you think I joined the Customs division? Guys, I was born and grew up here. You can't do *anything* without CLARA knowing. The only reason most people join Customs is to have a little excitement, you know? But even then, you have to work your way up to the top to have the *real* fun, yeah?"

Tara's face dropped. "But then, you're so busy dealing with all the admin, training and management tasks, you don't have any time for fun. I have been waiting years to meet some smugglers to finally get to have some excitement!" Tara grinned mischievously and raised an eyebrow. "Talking of excitement, you two must be doing it like, all the time yeah? With the adrenaline and excitement, and cooped up in a tiny metal box for weeks on end?"

"Er... we're professional partners, if that's what you're asking. I'm the pilot and engineer, he deals with the business side."

Tara giggled with obvious glee. "Oooh, and what business have you brought here then?"

Higgs kept silent.

"Oh no, Mr Dittum, we're not recording any more. It's fine." ...

"I ONLY HEAR WHAT I WANT TO, TO MAKE SURE EVERYTHING IS FINE."

Soap nudged Higgs with her elbow and nodded towards Tara.

"Oh yeah, well we are right in the middle of quite a dangerous job actually..."

"Please, please tell me!"

Higgs proceeded to tell Tara about the last few days, up to and including the tall stranger being jettisoned from Morley Station. She said nothing the whole time, completely focused on his story.

"Ah. I think your man has followed you here. To the surface at least."

"Wha-at? And I thought I kicked his tont real good! He just doesn't give up that one. You gonna go after him with guns?"

Tara put her hands up. "Oh no, I'm not going up there. No-one is. We'll just let our killer robots deal with him."

"Ki... killer robots?"

"Yes, we have them stationed all throughout the City. Armed with energy rifles and stun grenades. They're fantastic!"

"I don't remember hearing about them before."

"Oh yeah, we brought them in some months ago. The litter situation was getting out of hand."

"Wow."

A thought crossed Tara's mind as her brow furrowed. "So, how can you be sure your data cards are missing again?"

"The nan... na... nanonymous tip-off you got. It had to be someone after the data card. I bet, if you check that list of our possessions, you won't find any data cards on it."

Tara immediately tapped at the holoscreen and flicked through the list.

"You're right! Oh my word. We've got a thief in the department! Someone sneaking around fingering our takings, like a hot lover hiding inside a sweaty wardrobe. I won't stand for this."

She started tapping at the air and a series of video images appeared. "If someone took your cards, they will be on this surveillance footage."

Higgs tried to stretch his arm but couldn't. "Hey, I don't suppose you could loosen these straps a little could you? I think I'm getting cramp."

Tara gave him an odd look. "But you just did."

"Oh good grief, here too?"

"SAFETY ABOVE COMFORT. BECAUSE YOU DO NOT KNOW WHAT YOU ARE DOING."

"Fair enough CLARA."

"Got him!" Tara spun the screen round to show Higgs and Soap a blue haired man pocketing both their data cards from the boxes of items being taken off their ship. "Do you recognise him?"

"No. Shouldn't you?"

"That's just it, I don't. I know the names and faces of every person in the department. This man is an impostor."

She spun the screen back round and sent out a message.

"Right. His face is on every officials' HUD display and programmed into every killer robot. He won't get far."

"Miss Brissoles, we really appreciate your help with this."

"Are you kidding? This is the most fun I've had in years! But... it doesn't come for free."

"Whatcha want?" said Soap.

"One of the supposed perks of being a Customs officer is you get first dibs on all the confiscated stuff. But, like I mentioned earlier, no smugglers ever come here. Unless..."

Higgs knew that was his cue. "Unless someone you happened to know was allowed to bring in some goods now and again, as long as you and your team got a... preview, shall we say?"

Tara grinned. "Exactly. And anything else that happened to be in your hold wouldn't really be our concern."

"Miss Brissoles, I think we have a deal."

Tara tapped at the screen one final time and the restraints around their arms and legs clicked open and flicked back into the chairs. Higgs and Soap stood up, rubbing their arms.

"Right, once we get that blue haired man, and the data cards, I'll contact you two. Unless you find him first of course, which he might prefer to being filled with holes like a sponge by our killer robots. One restriction though, you can't leave the upper concourse. I'm afraid that's programmed into CLARA because you've been a 'guest' of the department."

"I'm never going to see those gardens."

"Apparently there's going to be light drizzle today," said Tara.

"Drizzle! Do you hear that Soap, drizzle!"

"Aw, I'm sorry Higgs."

"OUR GARDENS OUR REALLY QUITE LOVELY."

"Thanks CLARA."

CHAPTER 19

bing dong
**"WELCOME TO VARDA CITY ONE, THE MOST
SURVEILLED CITY IN THE GALAXY, FOR YOUR
SAFETY AND PUNISHMENT."**

Higgs shook the cheery voice out of his head and tried to focus on his HUD as he and Soap wandered through a busy shopping area. The sunlight bouncing down from the collectors above them was bright and warm, and the citizens were all out doing their consumerist duty for the good of the city.

"You found it yet?"

Higgs ignored her and placed a marker on his HUD before striding off across a small bridge and through a park.

"You found it yet?"

"Nope. I told you, the nanotracker is a really old cheap one. It doesn't have much power. The only thing it can do is send a ping back when you look for it. We need to move around the concourse and triangulate it. You know, the old fashioned way, like sea pirates used to do."

Soap's face lit up. "I love sea pirates! I downloaded all the stories about sea pirates I could find on the DataNet when I was a kid. Of course, some of them turned out to be ancient stories about computer software before it all went open source. And some were about pirates that liked to go bare chested all the time and preferred riding ladies to riding the waves. But in any case, I read them over and over."

They left the park and entered an area of restaurants underneath a group of skyscrapers, people sat outside chatting over their drinks.

"I wanted to be a lady pirate, docking into strange ports, spearing blackguards and ramming vessels. And sometimes I wanted to be the lady pirate the bare chested pirates were..."

"Got it! This way!"

Soap followed Higgs and some minutes later they were standing in an open area near some construction hardware shops.

"OK, this is where the data card triangulates to."

Soap looked around. "But there's nothing here?"

"Yeah, because I'm pinging it to be three hundred and ten metres away. Below us."

They both stared down at the ground.

"But Tara said we can't leave the concourse level. If we do, we really *will* be going to prison. I don't think she can override CLARA for that one."

Higgs rubbed his chin. "Well, the nearest access to the lower levels is just behind us, next to the circular tram stop."

"We can't go down there."

Higgs flicked up the public map of the city on his HUD.

"And directly underneath that is the Honsey Market. Then below that is an emergency refuge area for solar flare radiation bursts..."

"We can't go down there."

"Then we have various engineering, structural, yadda yadda, before we get to the restricted areas above the energy recirculation plant and the giant siphons that drop down into the depths of the tube."

"We can't go down there."

"And from the tracker, it looks as if the data card is somewhere in the engineering section – Structural Support T-04."

"We're going down there, aren't we?"

"Absolutely."

"I just knew it." Soap put her head in her hands. "Look, if you're going to do it, and you totally are, why don't you just hack her or something?"

"Oh no, no, no." Higgs waved a finger at her. "You don't hack an AI. An AI hacks *you*!"

Soap put her face in his and stared him down. "You what?"

"Auto-drives and maintenance robots are one thing, but you do *not* try and hack a supervisor AI. Let me put it this way... when I was in school we used to have hacking competitions at break time. You know, the standard thing: first to hack the Pensival Shopping Centre and set the fee for the toilets to a thousand credits, first to get into the school attendance records and replace all the staff images with pictures of front tonts... but then one kid, Overly Jones, decided to go one better. A new AI had gone online that controlled the Captain Williams City transport system. He thought it would be fun to go in and subtract a minute from each departure time. He almost did it too..."

Higgs face turned serious and Soap put a hand on his shoulder. "What happened?"

"He got as far as the main display interface for all the departure boards. If he couldn't actually change the times, he was going to alter the boards, just to confuse people. But the AI found him. You see, when you hack a 'dumb' system, there are layers of safety switches, locks and traps that are all designed to protect the system. Sometimes they will try and track you, but that's not really the point of them. They're designed to be passive. But when you hack a supervisor AI... they take it personally. The AI retaliated. Sent a massive autonomous data burst back to track down the source. It did. It fried his implants instantly."

"Oh no."

"The AI had no way of knowing it was just a kid doing this. An adult would have just needed a reboot, painkillers and some prison time. But he was in hospital for days, had his whole implant system replaced, months of therapy, but he was never the same after that. Parts of his memory, his personality, were gone forever. So if school taught me nothing else, it's that you *never* mess with a supervisor AI."

"So what are we going to do?"

Higgs turned round to look at the tram stop. "All we need is a way down there that CLARA won't spot..."

"She has eyes everywhere."

"...or won't follow."

With that thought, Higgs ran over to a railing and looked over. Directly below him he saw a mass of pipes and cabling. Below that was a mesh of metalwork. Below that there was the roof of a building, steam.

"That's no good."

Higgs ran over to the tram stop. Soap jogged after him. He crossed the tracks to the far platform and leaned over the railing there. Below him was mostly metalwork and a sheer drop into the heart of the planet.

"Better. Hey, Soap? I've got an idea."

"Oh foob."

(Twenty minutes later)

"Higgs, don't do it! It's not worth it!"

"You can't stop me Soap! I'm going to do it!"

Higgs was wobbling on the top of the railings, one hand steadying himself on a metal support. Soap stood a few feet away, keeping the small crowd of onlookers back, including the three transport staff who had come over to help.

"Please Sir, come down from there. We can talk this through."

"Oh can we? Are you a financial expert? A business lawyer perhaps? No? Then you can't help at all."

"Higgs, it's just one bad deal. We lost a bit of money on it, but we'll get more work. It's not worth throwing yourself into oblivion for."

The crowd murmured in agreement.

"But there's more Soap. Things I haven't told you. There are loans, debts I hid from you. The truth is, there *is* no business any more."

The crowd gasped.

"What? What do you *mean* Higgs?"

Soap scanned the crowd. It was four people deep now and even the tram drivers had stopped to have a look, their passengers pressing themselves up against the windows.

"My business, my *life* is ruined. RUINED!" Higgs sobbed uncontrollably.

The crowd went "oh" and an old lady started crying.

"We can work it out together Higgs. You and me, just like we always have."

The crowd went "yeah" and nodded. Soap spotted the sleek, and slightly curved rectangular head of a killer robot nudging its way through to the front of the crowd. Now she knew for sure CLARA was watching.

"It's too late Soap. TO-OOO LA-AATE! Why? WHY!"

"OK Higgs, it's time. I mean... it's time you came down from there and... and into my arms."

The crowd went "aww".

Higgs spotted the robot as it appeared next to the station guards. Its bulky chest, with its arms folded in at the sides, pushed the men out of the way as it rolled to a stop on its cluster of ball wheels.

"But there's nothing left for me here! I may as well throw myself into this deep abyss that you could never find or recover a body from. I mean, I wouldn't even bother looking personally, I'd just assume they were gone forever. No need to check or anything."

"Higgs, your business might be a tattered scrim sack but you have the rest of your life left to somehow work your way back from utter devastation."

Higgs let go of the support.

"You've always been good to me Soap. I just wanted to thank you for all your help. Your final month's salary is in your account. Good luck with the rest of your life."

"But Higgs, I love you!"

"I know."

Higgs let himself fall backwards off the railing.

Soap screamed and leapt towards him, managing to grab him round the waist, their momentum taking them both over the edge. The crowd gasped in horror. Some turned away or pressed their faces into the chests of their loved ones.

The three station guards didn't need to look over the railing to know that the strange couple would now be spending the next ten minutes tumbling down the tube until they burned up. They decided to disperse the crowd, keeping the trams running. Later they would have a three-way game of rock paper scissors to decide who was going to fill in the incident report form.

The killer robot thought to itself, **"THAT WAS ODD,"** before making its way to an access lift to the lower levels.

CHAPTER 20

"I thought that was pretty convincing," said Higgs, as the two of them swung upside down by the rope tied to his ankle.

"It convinced me!"

Soap was clinging on to him, arms and legs wrapped round his body.

"Told you nobody would notice the rope. It's all about misdirection you see."

"Ya know, I'm not the best with heights Higgs. Not, like, phobia strength or anything, but I prefer to be able to see the ground."

"Really? I never knew that. How do you deal with flying in space then?"

"'Cos there's no 'down' in space, dummy."

"Well, whatever you do, don't look down. Well, up, technically. You know what I mean."

Soap took a few breaths to steady herself, then unwrapped her legs and let herself swing the right way up. With a few kicks of her legs she swung them towards the nearest support, and hooked her foot around it.

"Grab on!"

Higgs clutched onto the support and started climbing 'downwards' up it, until he was able to turn himself the right way up and dig his free foot into a gap to support himself. He untied the brand new hardware store rope from his ankle and shimmied down to where Soap was already leaping between beams towards a wider walkway next to a fence. By the time Higgs had (rather more slowly) navigated the beams, she had already forced open a security gate and they both quickly ducked through it.

After a detour through some store rooms, they found themselves in the Honsey Market area. It was a huge market, stretching as far as they could see in all directions from where they stood. This sub-level had about ten metres height between it and the one above, allowing up to three floors of buildings. And they were stacked tightly next to each other, with gangways and ladders leading up and down to hundreds of small shops and stalls. It was also busy, with thick crowds pushing through the narrow passageways. Soap immediately wished she was back on the top level again, then got distracted by the smell of street food and tried to locate the source with just her nose.

Higgs brought up his HUD and pinged the nanotracker. "It's three floors below us. Let's keep to the busy areas and keep our faces down, should be harder for CLARA to spot us here. If she's still bothering to look that is."

Soap nodded and they made their way down a wide metal stairwell, lined with street sellers trying to flog cheap toys. The further they went down, the more surprised they were to find people still here. The "Underlevels" of Varda City One weren't much known to visitors, but comprised almost one fifth of the total population. They were generally left alone by the security and killer robots as long as they didn't jeopardise the city structure or get into too much trouble. Also there were now too many of them to really do anything about, bar a huge, costly, and likely unpopular security operation.

Down here people lived on the rubbish from above, borrowed light from craftily placed mirror set-ups and hidden from radiation bursts in their own handmade shelters. They scavenged what they could from the city's giant rubbish skips, an ear always out for the alarm that meant they had thirty seconds to scramble to safety before the trapdoor was released and the contents were dumped into the tube below them. They had built outwards from the support frame, small ramshackle houses teetering over the abyss, held on by used bolts, cheap rope and a lot of luck. Some people have dreams they are falling which wakes them up, here it was a real world hazard.

They also had their own version of the Honsey Market, but slightly more illegal. It was here that Higgs and Soap finally found themselves, moving slowly through a rather more ragged looking crowd. Not that Higgs had noticed, he was too focused on his HUD.

"OK. The data card is twenty metres away, straight ahead."

They moved through the crowd as vendors shouted their wares, most of it junk or fruit and vegetables stolen from the farms above.

Soap sniffed the air. "I smell data card."

"Eh?"

"You know how you get to know the smell of something after a while?"

"Not really."

"Well, it's close."

Higgs checked his HUD. "OK, it's now ten metres away. Uh... behind us."

They spun round and walked back the way they came.

"It's... still ten metres away... hang on, I don't get it."

Soap elbowed him in the ribs. "There."

She pointed to a blue haired man walking a few people in front of them. "That's the guy from the Customs surveillance footage."

It didn't seem the thief had spotted them as he walked purposefully but calmly away from the market area and down a series of narrow passages, walkways and down a ladder, without looking back once. They kept a good distance behind and saw him go up to a door on a ramshackle three storey structure, jammed so tightly between a service platform and a series of beams it looked as if it had become stuck under a low bridge while being moved. Here, the blue haired man *did* look around, before unhooking a latch and going inside.

Higgs and Soap hid behind a set of thick water pipes.

"Is he going to meet his buyer?"

As they pondered what to do next, a group of five Grey Dragons appeared from another direction. The glasses Dragon, still bruised and swollen from his beating on Morley Station, and now missing his cybernetic arm, unlatched the door and all five went in.

"How did he get off Morley?"

"I'm sure that's an interesting tale for Barty to tell us the next time we're there."

"So, we wait until the deal is done, then jump 'em?"

"Seems like the outcome most likely to end in death, so why not?"

"Wait..."

A group of seven huge muscular guys in combats appeared from the same direction the Grey Dragons came from. They all had a diagonal line of hair running across their head. Higgs and Soap had no idea whether any of these guys were the same ones from Clarissa or Morley Station, they all looked so similar. The lead guy tried to open the door a few times, before he spotted the latch and angrily snapped it off. They all disappeared inside.

"OK. This is going to be interesting. I'm guessing our blue haired thief wasn't hired by either of these gangs, but thought he would start a bidding war between them and cash in."

"Shame he doesn't know they don't really get on."

"In *way* over his head."

"Yeah, not like us. We've got this all planned out."

"Actually... we have. We wait until this lot have 'sorted things out' between them, pick off the survivors and grab the data card."

As they watched, a tall thin figure in a long dark coat walked towards the building. They stayed silent and hidden, peering between the pipes, but he turned and looked directly at them through his dark goggles. He lifted up his arm, pointed a long finger at them, then disappeared inside.

"That clinches it. We're going in."

"Into the building with all the shouting and screaming coming from inside?"

Higgs listened to all the shouting and screaming coming from inside. It went on for some time.

"Well, you know what they say: In for a penny..."

"In for a pounding!"

They ran out from behind the pipes towards the building and flattened themselves either side of the door. Soap counted to three on her fingers then they flung the door open and ran in.

There were a surprising number of people still left alive, all fighting around the body of the blue haired thief slumped against a pillar, data card still clutched between his fingers. The tall stranger was trying to fight his way through the throng but he looked injured, burned, and one of his blades had snapped off. Not only that, the gangs weren't giving anyone an inch this time round.

"You know, in hindsight, we should have grabbed it off our blue haired friend when we spotted him earlier. Would have involved less imminent death."

"I'll take the guy in black."

"I'll take the hiding in the corner."

"Let's do this."

"INTERRUPT ILLEGAL ACTIVITY!"

Everybody froze and turned to look at Higgs and Soap. Higgs and Soap froze and turned to look at the killer robot standing in the doorway.

"THANK YOU FOR YOUR COMPLIANCE. DEATH FOLLOWS!"

The tall figure quickly leapt out of a back window into the abyss as the remaining men all said "Killer robot!" in unison.

The robot drew its arms arms out of the grooves in the side of its torso, revealing the gun barrels on the ends, which it pointed into the room. Moment later, blasts of energy shot out. Higgs and Soap could only scream and cower in fear, uselessly covering themselves with their arms as the bursts of hot plasma sizzled in the air around them, tearing limbs from their associated joints.

After just under eight seconds of constant noise, the firing stopped. The robot spun its arms round twice and re-holstered them at the side of its torso. There was complete silence as the hot, acrid smoke slowly cleared to reveal a room devoid of life. Devoid of life apart from Higgs and Soap crouching in the middle of it. It took them both a few seconds to register they were still alive, before they carefully stood up. Higgs looked around, regretted it instantly and covered his face with his hands.

"Oh the horror!"

"IT IS A SHAME YOUR DISRUPTIVE BEHAVIOUR MADE US KILL THOSE WHO DID NOT VALUE THE SHARED GOALS OF OUR CITY."

Higgs peered through his fingers at the churned up mess of body parts that decorated the room.

"That told them CLARA."

Soap checked herself over to make sure her fur hadn't been caramelised. "Why... why are we still alive CLARA?"

"THIS... THIS..." there was a noise like someone bumped into a microphone, then Tara's voice spoke from the kiiler robot unit. "Hello? Can you hear me?"

"Tara! Yes. Yes, we hear you. Did you do this?"

"Those other guys arrived in the city while you were in custody. We had been monitoring their movements for a while, but lost them when they converged on the Underlevels. I figured it must have something to do with your missing data card. Too much of a coincidence otherwise. When I spotted your 'swan dive' off the railings (nicely done by the way, that was really class), I updated our system to tell it you were Customs informants. That way CLARA wouldn't kill you, whatever happened."

"YOU ARE OF MORE USE ALIVE THAN DEAD. UNTIL YOU ARE OF NO USE."

"Thanks CLARA," said Higgs and Soap.

"And, let's just say I don't like to be indebted to anyone. You helped track down some nasty types that slipped through our net. Could have been embarrassing for us if they had caused trouble. But in finding you, we found them, so in return, I saved your lives. I'd say we're mutually satisfied, like a pair of hot lovers bringing each other to..."

"So we're OK to go?"

"Yes indeed. Freedom of the City and all that. Although you might want to pick those bits of brain off yourselves first..."

Higgs fainted.

CHAPTER 21

Higgs and Soap looked up at the building in front of them. It was silver grey, like all the other skyscrapers in the commercial area of the upper concourse, with a grid of black windows across all four sides. It wasn't one of the largest buildings here, some were twice as tall, but all were dwarfed by the massive Spire in the background. Their eyes drifted back down to the entrance and the large "Harper Intergalactic Logistics" sign above it.

Soap whispered in Higgs' ear. "You sure this is the place?"

"Well, it's the address our client gave us. We're to go to the twenty eighth floor and the receptionist there will be expecting us."

"I smell something not quite right."

Higgs thought quietly for a moment. "I must admit, he seemed surprised to hear from me, and even more so that we had the data card."

"Maybe word got round about our... various delivery issues. Probably thought we were dead."

"So did I at several points," Higgs sighed. "What the heck. We need the job, we need the money."

"And if it all goes munty in there, at least they might ship our bodies back home."

"That would be nice of them."

They went inside the building, admiring the décor, and made their way to the lifts. On the twenty eighth floor, they stepped out into a large, sparse waiting area. It had a single, long bench on one side and a small oval desk with a woman sat behind it at the other. She smiled as they approached her and she gestured towards the long wall in front of them. Higgs and Soap looked puzzled, and the woman gestured again.

"Hmm yes, lovely wall. Looks solid, doesn't it Soap?"

"Yeah, very solid. Almost like we can't walk through it or something."

The woman gestured again, more forcefully this time. They shrugged at each other and walked towards the wall. As they did, a square section slowly became translucent. Then lines appeared in it in the shape of two doors, which peeled apart as they approached.

"Hey! This is a nanotech wall! CLARA wouldn't be very happy if she knew about this." Higgs winked at the woman, who gave him a blank stare in return. "We'll just go in then."

The other side of the wall was an office, the same size as the waiting area. Directly ahead was a window the width of the building, looking out over the city and The Spire. Between them and the window sat two small seats, a large desk and a huge office chair, its back turned to them. Somebody was sat in it, but said nothing until the doors sealed shut behind them.

"Higgs and Soap. I must admit, the two of you have far surpassed my expectations. Then again..." the chair spun round "...they weren't particularly high to begin with."

Sat in front of them was a young man in a dark blue suit, silver hair brushed back sleekly. Not quite sure how to take his comment, Higgs erred on the side of customer service.

"Well that's Higgs & Soap: Galaxy Delivery for you. We always like to go that extra light year for our clients!"

The man burst out laughing and sat back in his chair so hard it started to turn round again. Higgs could hear Soap quietly growling and gently put a hand on her forearm. "I got this," he whispered. Regaining control of himself, the man swivelled back round.

"Oh, you two have been nothing if not entertaining. I've been watching your exploits pop up on the police and security channels over the last couple of days. I'm amazed you're still in one piece! And of course, you still have the goods?"

"Absolutely."

Higgs reached into his breast pocket and pulled out the data card.

"Excellent!" The man stood up and reached across his desk.

Higgs and Soap didn't move.

"Normally we don't care much about the details of a job beyond the pick up and drop off, but given the 'entertaining exploits' we've had to go through to get, and keep, hold of this for you..."

"And stay alive," interrupted Soap.

"...and stay alive, I think we're owed *some* kind of explanation, Mr...?"

The man stood up and smiled. "Of course. You're absolutely correct. I must apologise for my rudeness. My name is Mr Harper. I own and run Harper Intergalactic Logistics. And this..." he gestured to the wall behind them as it transformed into two doors again, "is Mr Reeves."

The doors opened and the tall figure in the black coat and goggles swept in. He glowered at Higgs and Soap as the door disappeared behind him.

Soap extended her claws and jumped between him and Higgs. "You again! Right, Higgs, Mr Harper get behind the desk and DO NOT let that data card out of your sight. We're not losing it at the last minute! Come on Mr Tall, Dark and Radiation Burnt, let's see what you've got left."

The man made fists, ready to flick his blades out, but instead just stood there and muttered, "One day. One day."

Mr Harper started chuckling and walked out from behind his desk, waving his hands in the air. He stepped between Soap and the figure like a referee breaking up a fight. "No, no. Stop, please.

CHAPTER 21

You've got it all wrong. He works for *me* you fools!"

Higgs and Soap both stood, mouths agape. "You what? How were *we* supposed to know?" said Soap.

"There were so many people after us it got confusing after a while."

"And if he works for you, why the heck was he trying to kill *us*?"

"And why didn't you just use him to get the data here in the first place? Why hire us?"

"All valid questions, deserving of an answer. Please, let's just sit down and I'll explain everything. Please." He motioned to the two small seats at the front of his desk and went back to his chair. Soap took some convincing, but sat down next to Higgs as Mr Reeves joined Mr Harper at the other side of the desk. The cyborg stood behind him, hands behind his back. They couldn't see his eyes through his dark goggles, but they knew he was eyeballing them the whole time.

Mr Harper took a while to gather his thoughts, then he clasped his hands together and started to talk.

"I have built a good business here. I am only twenty two years old, younger than both of you, and yet I have a small delivery empire stretching like a web across the whole galaxy."

Higgs thought the comparison was slightly unnecessary, but let him continue all the same.

"And yet, I am destined for more. I have always known I was destined for more. I just could never prove it."

He turned the chair and pointed out of the window towards another skyscraper. It was the same silver grey but was clad in blue glass and was over twice as tall, with a giant "T" logo at the top. It was also one of the architects' more vertiginous designs, seemingly supported over the void by only two small arches of metal.

"See that? That's Tosen Transport. The CEO, Mr Garrick Tosen, recently died and his oldest son, Jarrick, only twenty, became the new owner. As his oldest son, he was his rightful heir to the business."

He turned back round to face them. "Except he wasn't."

"Whatcha mean he wasn't?"

Mr Harper looked down at his desk, a sudden look of sadness on his face.

"I have these memories... no, to be precise, I *had* memories of a happy childhood. They were wiped from me."

Soap's ears dropped.

"I was eleven when I was kidnapped by a squad of men and taken to some dark room near the bottom of the city. They injected me with gene altering drugs then hooked me to a machine. They proceeded to destroy any memory of my life up to that point, replacing it with the most bland, generic upbringing you can imagine. They then dumped me at this house in the core rock levels.

CHAPTER 21

This was supposed to be my home, they were supposed to be my parents, this was supposed to be my life. But I knew it was wrong. I always knew. I don't know whether the wiping process didn't work properly, or my memories were too strong, but I always had ghosts of the past inside me."

"That's terrible!"

"My surrogate parents were lovely, and looked after me well, but I knew they weren't mine. Maybe they had a son who died and I was the replacement, or maybe they were just good actors paid well. I don't know. Even now I can't ask them. Considering the years of love and care they have given me, it would be unfair of me to say anything. But I always knew I was in the wrong place. I always knew I was destined for more. And this drove me to succeed. It drove me to be better than who my memories told me I was. It drove me to find out who my real parents were. And then one day, I found out..."

He held out his hand to Higgs. Higgs didn't delay in handing over the data card to him. Mr Harper turned the card over in his fingers.

"I found the room they took me to. I found who owned it when I was eleven. A shell company. I had medical tests which confirmed my DNA had been deliberately altered to disguise my true heritage. I tracked every piece of information I could find, and it all led back to Garrick Tosen."

Higgs and Soap gasped.

"People were afraid to talk of course. Mr Tosen had a fierce reputation for silencing anyone speaking out of line, but I did find some willing to speak up. Some of the old staff at his penthouse recognised me, despite the alteration. Told me about an older son, Merrick, who just disappeared one day. They were told not to mention him to anyone, otherwise they would lose more than their pension. So Merrick just ceased to exist. Except he didn't." Harper tapped the side of his head, "He was still in here."

Soap gave a quiet "Yay!"

"And other than the bad wiping, they made one more mistake. They made hard copies of everything. Mr Tosen was old school, didn't trust new tech much, always like to keep a physical copy. For business..." he placed the data card on a faint square on the desk, "and for family."

A holoscreen appeared on the side wall and everyone turned to look at the display.

"Now Mr Dittum, you *did* open every single file and look at them, didn't you?"

"If I say 'yes' is that a 'no problem, I was expecting you to do that' yes, or a 'I'll have to kill you for doing that' yes?"

"No, it's fine. Everyone will know soon enough. This..." the screen zoomed in on an image of a hand written letter, "I wrote to my father, Mr Tosen when I was eight years old. It was part of that ancient history learning project they make you do where they force you to actually write words with your hands using a physical implement."

"I did that too!" piped up Soap. "Did you ever find out why it's called a 'double-you' instead of a 'double-vee'?"

"Haha, no, I never did! Utterly pointless exercise. But nevertheless, it led to this image being taken by my father. This image of a letter where I told him how much I loved him, and how I wanted to grow up to be a no-nonsense businessman like him. To make him proud."

Higgs and Soap sniffed back tears as Harper flicked through photos of Mr Garrick and his, very obviously, two sons. They were playing in a large roof garden, splashing water at each other in a swimming pool, lying asleep on a sofa, exhausted from play. Then he opened a short video clip from Mr Tosen's implant view, which showed him and his mother lying on sun loungers by the pool, while two boys tried to creep up on them from the side with a bucket of water. He knew they were there, but he let them douse him in water, then play-chased them round the pool before grabbing them both, one under either arm, and leaping into the water.

The video ended.

"I would have thought he would have scolded us both for that, being such an angry man. But he didn't. He had a playful, loving side. A fatherly side. You know... I go over it in my head all the time, but to this day, I don't know why he did what he did to me. Maybe he loved Jarrick more?

Maybe he didn't want two sons squabbling over the business, damaging his share price. I just don't know. And now he's dead, I guess I never will."

Mr Harper banged on the table, turning off the video feed in the process. A startled Higgs and Soap wiped tears from their faces as they looked across the desk.

"But it doesn't matter, and I don't care. All that matters now is that I have proof. A certified physical copy of the data from the Clarissa Digital Archives as evidence. The raw data on its own wouldn't have been sufficient you see. This hard copy has been stored by and can be tracked directly to Garrick Tosen. My Father."

Mr Harper stood up and walked over to the window, pointing at the blue skyscraper again.

"THAT business is mine!"

"Mr Harper?" asked Higgs.

"Yes?"

Higgs was still sniffing. "I mean, I'm sorry about what happened to you, and I'm really glad this evidence proves everything but... why hire us to get this for you? Why not just get your killer cyborg guy here to do the job?"

Mr Harper smiled. "There's no point taking over a business without knowing who on the inside has a knife out for you. If I had used Mr Reeves here, then I would have had the data within hours no doubt. But I would not have known which parties inside Tosen Transport and my *own* company were conspiring to keep my identity hidden. Thanks to you two, I tracked down who hired the Grey Dragons, The Beat Mob, Swift Fred/Rick and Blue Dave to make sure the data card never reached me. These people are now on my 'list' of who to clear out as soon as I claim the company for myself. Mr Reeves here was a backup plan, in case you didn't make it or if it looked as if the data card could be lost or destroyed."

"So, we were mole *and* shark bait, as well as your delivery service?"

"I'm afraid so."

"Well in that case, our price has doubled!"

Mr Harper laughed. "I'll pay you triple. Mainly out of genuine surprise you're still alive."

"Triple? Well, that covers our expenses and more." Higgs stood up and offered a hand. "Despite being in constant fear of our lives, it has been a pleasure doing business with you." They shook hands. "And I genuinely wish you the best of luck."

Soap stood up and offered her hand too. Mr Harper took it. "Yeah, you go show those bastards quite literally who's boss."

"I intend to."

"Oh, and getcha guy here some new clothes so he doesn't look like a background character from an ancient video game."

There was a metallic slicing noise as Mr Reeves extended one of his blades behind his back.

"Mr Reeves, please! Honestly, I've never known him to bear a personal grudge in all the years we've worked together. You must have really gotten under his skin. Anyhow, my assistant, Ms Bellweather, will deal with your payment. Thank you once again for your work. You two... really are quite special."

Higgs beamed. "That's what my mother always used to say to me."

"Oh, I'm sure she did."

⇐•⇒

Higgs and Soap stood outside Harper Logistics in the reflected sunlight, one successfully completed job under their belt and some much needed money in their account.

"You know Soap, I think we've done a good thing today."

"Yeh. This is the first job we've done where I can say I feel happy we've delivered something that won't result in a colossal loss of life."

"Even though, ironically, it almost cost us our *own* lives!" chuckled Higgs.

"I'm not comfortable with that irony."

"Me neither." Higgs took a deep breath in and looked up at the light bouncing down from the underside of the landing flower. "You know what I want to do now Soap?"

"Wash this blood off our clothes?"

"Exactly."

They nodded at each other and started looking for somewhere to stay.

EPILOGUE

"And in Varda City One Business news, less than four days after its sudden takeover by the unknown older son of its previous CEO, Tosen Transport has declared itself insolvent. The first task of the receivers will be to determine the cause of a so-called financial 'black hole' at the company. Initial suspicion is that Tosen Transport had long been puffing up its profits with dummy accounts to make it look like it was in the black, allowing it to apply for credit. However, a secret insider source tells us that these accounts did indeed exist, but were kept off the systems as they may have involved shipments of contraband goods. New CEO Merrick Tosen is helping city officials with their enquiries while his younger brother and previous CEO, Jarrick Tosen, is still missing, presumed to be on the run. Here is a message from CLARA."

"ILLEGAL ACTIVITY IS ITS OWN REWARD. AND WHEN IT IS NOT, INCARCERATION AT OUR PLEASURE IS."

"Thanks CLARA, and now for the radiation forecast…"

⇐•⇒

It had been a week since Higgs and Soap had delivered the data card, and in that time they had decided to stay in Varda City to see the gardens, make sure Tara gave them back their full inventory (she did, and it didn't take long), and to see how the takeover of Tosen Transport panned out.

Higgs had spent the time paying off his own debts and using the cash to buy some ads on the SubNet. If he had learned anything over the course of this job, it's that people liked free things. So he offered the first ten takers a free one-way delivery of anything to anywhere. They were gone in minutes. Then dozens more jobs came in after that. So many that, after he worked out the itinerary, they would have a full hold for the next ten galactic months.

Surprisingly, most of the business was from Varda City One itself. He heard from his contacts that a large delivery company, used by most customers to shift contraband items, was going through a surprise takeover. And it turned out that the smuggling business doesn't like uncertainty. Everyone was suddenly spooked that their lines of commerce might be disrupted and were looking to switch. And it just so happened that when they went on the SubNet looking for a replacement, they saw a "one free delivery" offer from a small delivery firm. A firm that, they'd heard on the grapevine, had just done a major delivery job in the city. A major delivery job, right under the noses of Customs, whilst pursued by some of the most violent gangs and thieves in the whole quadrant who all ended up dead. Impressive stuff.

As for that large delivery firm, Higgs never found out the name.

"Business is business. I guess you make your own fate after all," shrugged Higgs as he buckled himself into the co-pilot seat.

Soap finished plotting coordinates. "Cargo all secured down there?"

"Sure is. I've never seen it so full! Didn't I tell you business would pick up?"

"Yeah, but don't forget ten of those are free ones."

"But the other twenty aren't. Then we've got two to pick up on Morley Station before we head off to Hemnar Junction and from there..." he spread his arms wide, "the galaxy is ours!"

"You know you're going to have to spend the next ten months trapped in here with me," said Soap as she engaged flight systems and fired up the engines.

"There's nowhere I'd rather be."

Higgs held out a fist. Soap gave him a paw bump.

"So, what are we going to do for ten months..." Higgs scratched the back of his neck.

"Dead animal! Bird!" said Soap.

"Oh, oh... that's 'Cheep!'"

"Your turn."

Higgs looked sideways at Soap, a cheeky grin on his face.

"Cat?"

She smiled and gave a little giggle as she turned to look at him. "Meow!"

Soap lifted off from the landing petal, ascended the lava tube and blasted off into space.

ABOUT THE AUTHOR

Thank you for reading "Higgs & Soap: Galaxy Delivery". I hope you enjoyed my first attempt at a proper science fiction story, and a comedy one at that!

I had great fun writing it, coming up with crazy situations and daft names. But then the fun ended when I had to make sure it all made sense!

Thankfully Higgs and Soap themselves helped me along, their daft antics and banter lifting me through the difficult editing and formatting tasks.

I look forward to your thoughts and reviews, and here's hoping they will be back soon with more adventures!

Tony.

Tony Cooper was born and raised in Scotland. He studied Medicine before deciding to move into videogames instead. He worked at one of the largest UK game development and publishing companies in England for sixteen years and is now a science fiction author and freelance writer.

My Mailing List
   www.eepurl.com/biiEr1

My Blog
   www.hungryblackbird.com/thewormhole

Facebook
   www.facebook.com/TonyCooperAuthor

Twitter
   @_tonycooper

Email
   tonycooperauthor@gmail.com

Amazon
   www.amazon.com/author/tonycooper

Smashwords
   www.smashwords.com/profile/view/TonyCooper

Goodreads
   www.goodreads.com/user/show/7234993

OTHER TITLES

POWERLESS
The first book in the 'Powerless' series

When the best friend of a retired superhero is killed by another power, Martin must drag himself out of his self-imposed isolation to find out who is responsible. In doing so he finds himself digging up a past he would rather forget, risking exposing the secret of why the team split up and destroying all their lives in the process.

KILLING GODS
The second book in the 'Powerless' series

When the baby son of a physically mutated eighties villain goes missing from protective care, he goes on a rampage to try and find him.

In his way stand a Child Protection Officer following her heart above her duty, a violent anti-hero group desperate for media attention, a seemingly benevolent hero-worshipping cult and Martin and Hayley struggling to work out who they can trust.

THE RESURRECTION TREE AND OTHER STORIES
A collection of nine short stories about life, death and consequences.

A mix of creepy, disturbing contemporary fantasy and science fiction stories in one book.

Made in the USA
Charleston, SC
11 August 2015